As the twins stepped onto the wooden front porch, the second step creaked loudly, threatening to break beneath their weight.

"Well, Sooz, this is it," Chris said. With that, she stepped up to the front door, reached up for the tarnished brass knocker, and knocked three times.

Inside the house, the noise echoed. The girls stood on the porch for what seemed a very long time. They were surrounded by silence, except for the occasional chirping of a bird or the soft rushing sound of the wind blowing through the autumn leaves that still clung to the stark black branches of the tall trees in Mr. Kirgley's yard.

"Maybe there's nobody inside," Chris whispered. "Maybe we should just forget all about this, turn around, and go back home and . . ."

Just then, there was a loud creaking sound as the heavy front door was pulled open. . . .

THE
LOLLIPOP
PLOT

Cynthia Blair

FAWCETT JUNIPER • NEW YORK

Library of Congress Catalog Card Number: 90-90294

ISBN 0-449-70377-0

Manufactured in the United States of America

First Edition: November 1990

One

"*There's no place like home!*" *exclaimed Christine* Pratt. She dropped her two heavy suitcases, stuffed to the very limit, in the entryway of her parents' home.

Her twin sister Susan came in right behind her, carrying the much more practical compact weekend bag she had carefully packed for the girls' four-day stay. She blinked a few times as she glanced around, as if she couldn't quite believe she were really back in the house in which she had grown up.

"I feel the exact same way," she agreed, sighing wistfully. "You know, Chris, I love traveling just as much as you do. And it's really, really great, living in a big city. But when it comes to feeling as if I really *belong*, there's no place like Whittington."

"And we're glad you feel that way." Mr. Pratt, the twins' father, was wearing a big grin as he came strid-

1

ing in from the den to greet them. "Welcome home, girls!"

The girls' mother wasn't far behind.

"Chris! Susan!" Mrs. Pratt cried as she came down the stairs, her cheeks flushed. Immediately she rushed over and gave both of her daughters a big hug. "I can hardly believe we haven't seen you two since September. What is it, two whole months?"

"Ten weeks and three days, to be exact," Susan informed her. "Oh, Mom! I've missed you so much!"

With that, she threw her arms around her mother and gave her another big hug, one that proved just how sincere her words were.

"Me, too," echoed Chris. "And I've missed you, too, Dad. Oh, we both have so much to tell you!"

It was no surprise that the Pratt twins had so much to tell their parents. That autumn, the girls had started attending school in New York City. Chris was a freshman at the University of New York, where she was taking courses to help prepare her for her long-term goal of becoming a lawyer. Susan, meanwhile, was at the Morgan School of Art, pursuing her lifelong dream of studying drawing and painting so that one day she could be a professional artist.

But continuing their education at brand-new schools was only part of it. For the first time ever, the Pratt twins were living away from their hometown, sharing a small apartment in Manhattan's Greenwich Village. And they were greatly enjoying their newfound independence. It was even more fun than they had ever dreamed, making new friends, exploring the different neighborhoods of New York—and, as usual, finding time for an occasional adventure.

Just then, another member of the Pratt family strolled in, looking a little bit surprised by the commotion. But as soon as he saw what it was all about, he wasted no time in showing the girls that he, too, was pleased to see them.

"Jonathan! Oh, Jonathan, I sure have missed you." Chris scooped up the cat that belonged to Susan and her and rubbed her face against his soft fur.

"I think he missed us, too," Susan observed, reaching over to pet his silky head. "I don't think he understands why we left him behind."

"Well, I'll explain it all to him the very first chance I get."

"Gosh," Chris went on with a sigh, "we have so much to tell you that I don't know where to begin!"

"I have an idea. Why don't you begin by taking off your coats and coming into the kitchen?" suggested Mrs. Pratt. "I've already put on a pot of tea, figuring you two would be exhausted after your plane trip home."

"We are a little bit tired," Chris admitted. "But we're excited, too. In fact, maybe we're even too excited to sit still long enough to drink a cup of tea!"

"Uh, oh," her father teased. "You'd better not be. Not when your mother spent the entire morning making a chocolate layer cake in celebration of your homecoming."

"Chocolate cake? Oh, yum!" Chris cried. Already she was bounding toward the kitchen.

Susan, meanwhile, preferred to walk into the next room more slowly, with her parents at her side.

"It looks as if you said the magic words," she said with a smile. "You know how crazy Chris is about your homemade chocolate cake, Mom!"

"It seems to me I've seen you put away a piece or two in your day," her father joked, putting his arm around her.

Susan laughed. "I certainly can't deny that. Oh, gee, it's great to be home, even if it is only for four short days. Whoever thought up the idea of Homecoming Weekend must have been a genius."

"And I just know that this is going to be the greatest Homecoming Weekend ever," Chris said as the others joined her in the kitchen. She couldn't help overhearing their conversation, even as she busily arranged cake plates, tea cups, napkins, forks, and spoons on the kitchen table for the impromptu little tea party that was about to take place. "According to the notices we've been getting from Kelly Johnson, the chairperson of Whittington High School's Homecoming Committee this year, there are going to be so many different events going on that I don't expect to find the time to *sleep*."

"Just as long as you find the time to *eat*," her twin sister commented jokingly. "But it looks as if that's not going to be a problem."

She gestured toward the chocolate cake sitting on the kitchen counter. It was perfect, like something out of a bakery window, except for one thing: there was a thick line running around part of one side, a telltale sign that someone had taken the liberty of helping herself to a free sample.

"I hope you don't plan to spend *all* your time with Homecoming events," said Mr. Pratt. He helped finish setting the table, then took a seat. "I mean, you girls will be here at home for four whole days. Let's see, there's the rest of today, Friday. Then there's Saturday, Sunday, and most of Monday, right? That's not much time, but I hope you'll manage to squeeze in at least *some* time for your old dad!"

"Don't forget me," Mrs. Pratt was quick to add. "I'm just as anxious as your father is to hear all about your first semester. Chris, how are you enjoying your freshman year of college? Susan, I can't wait to hear all about art school."

The Pratt sisters didn't need a second invitation. They launched into story after story about life in New York City, pausing only to devour not one but two huge slabs of chocolate cake each. They told their parents all about the friends they had made, the courses they were taking, the places they had seen. And of course Mr. and Mrs. Pratt were eager to hear the details of the twins' latest adventures.

Adventures, after all, had played a large part in both the Pratt twins' lives ever since they were sixteen years old. That was when Susan and Chris agreed to change places for two weeks, with Susan pretending to be Chris and Chris pretending to be Susan, so that each one of these two very different individuals could find out more about what the other's life was like.

It turned out to be easier than they ever dreamed.

Ordinarily the girls dressed so differently, wore their hair so differently, and used such different makeup that they hardly even looked like sisters, much less twins. But they were twins, identical twins, with the exact same shoulder-length chestnut brown hair, large brown eyes, and pert ski-jump noses. And so changing places worked. They nicknamed their little caper *The Banana Split Affair*, because the stakes for the bet they made with each other as to whether or not they could actually carry it off was a banana split. And much to their delight, it worked.

Once they had discovered that they could, indeed, take advantage of their identical appearances to do things that most other people simply couldn't manage, they went on to become involved in many more such schemes.

In *The Pink Lemonade Charade*, for example, they helped a Russian ballerina defect to the United States. In *The Double Dip Disguise*, they reunited two little girls with their real father while ferreting out the culprit behind the illegal dumping of toxic chemicals on a resort island. And in *The Popcorn Project*, they helped an aspiring actress escape the clutches of a desperate kidnapper, and in the process earned themselves a chance to be in a movie.

Interestingly enough, aside from their shared love of adventure, the two identical Pratt twins were actually very different. Susan was the more practical one. She was studious, cautious, and just a little bit shy. She preferred spending her time reading, daydreaming, and, especially nowadays, painting, drawing, and experimenting in all kinds of artistic media. Chris, meanwhile, was the social butterfly. She tended to take more risks and jump head first into things—that is, when her busy schedule afforded her the time.

Today, however, the girls were thinking about neither their similarities nor their differences. They weren't thinking about any of their past adventures, either. Instead, they were concentrating as hard as they could on their mother's homemade chocolate cake.

"I didn't realize until today just how much I've missed home cooking," Chris said with a contented sigh. She folded up her napkin and placed it beside her empty plate. Then she sat back in her chair and glanced around at the rest of her family, all seated around the kitchen table with her.

"I take it that your mother's cake was a success," teased Mr. Pratt. "Don't forget, I helped make the frosting. Your mother tells me I have the strongest stirring arm this side of Elmsford."

Just as Susan stood up to put away the rest of the cake, the doorbell rang. All four of the Pratts looked at each other, surprised.

"Goodness, who could that be?" asked Mrs. Pratt. "I'm certainly not expecting any visitors today."

"Well, it *is* Homecoming Weekend," Chris replied with a twinkle in her eye. "Just about everybody we know in the whole town of Whittington has come back. So it could be just about *anyone*." Already she was bounding toward the front door, anxious to see who their mysterious visitor was.

And when she flung open the front door, she wasn't at all disappointed.

"Katy!" she shrieked, throwing her arms around

one of her best friends from high school, someone she hadn't laid eyes on for almost three full months.

Katy Johnson was a petite girl with curly red hair, bright green eyes, a million freckles, and a bubbly, fun-loving nature. She had been a friend of the twins ever since kindergarten. She also happened to be one of the most accomplished athletes who had ever passed through Whittington High.

At the end of her senior year, in fact, she had been awarded a full scholarship to the state college in nearby Elmsford. There she was majoring in physical education, carrying a full course load as she worked toward becoming a gym teacher. She also found the time to win countless awards in all the local gymnastic competitions. As if all that weren't enough, Katy also held down a part-time job. Two evenings a week, plus Saturdays, she worked in the Children's Department of Marbury's Department Store at the Elmsford Mall.

"Hi, Chris!" Katy cried, returning the hug. "Oh, it's so great to see you. I missed you so much—and I want to hear all about everything that's happened to you since September."

"Everything?" Chris repeated in a teasing tone.

"Everything!" Katy insisted with a grin.

"Well, in that case, I sure hope you're not in a hurry!"

"Is that Katy's voice I hear?" Susan called in from the kitchen. She peeked out of the doorway, eager to see if she was right.

"It sure is." Chris was already heading back into

the kitchen with Katy in tow. Both girls had huge smiles on their faces.

"Come on in, Katy," said Mrs. Pratt. "What a lovely surprise."

"I'm so glad to see you!" said Susan, beaming. "And you're just in time for chocolate cake."

"Thanks. I'd love some, but I'm afraid I'm in training." Katy made a face. "There's a big all-county gymnastics meet next weekend, and I want to be in tip-top shape. In fact, the only sweets I allow myself these days are these!"

Wearing a mischievous grin, she reached into the pocket of her jacket and pulled out a handful of brightly colored lollipops.

"Lollipops?" Mr. Pratt asked, surprised.

"That's right," Katy replied. "It's a little trick of mine. I use them as kind of a reward. I always treat myself to one after I've had a rigorous workout. They're certainly easy enough to come by; we give them out to the kids at the department store. Over at Marbury's, we get them in by the boxful."

"Speaking of exercise," Katy went on, putting the lollipops back into her pocket, "I thought perhaps we could all catch up on one anothers' news while taking a bike ride."

"What a wonderful idea!" Susan exclaimed.

"Gee, I haven't been on a bicycle since we moved to New York City," Chris said. "I hope mine hasn't gotten rusty."

Chris's bicycle was still in excellent condition, she was pleased to discover, and a few minutes later she,

Katy, and Susan pedaled along one of the quiet residential lanes on the outer edge of Whittington. It was a crisp November day, perfect for a biking tour of an area they hadn't seen for weeks—and missed so much that just being there again was a real treat.

Meanwhile, the three girls chattered away, filling each other in on all the details of the first three months of their freshman year of college. Chris and Susan were full of tales of their new lives in New York City. For the second time that day, they found themselves telling an enthralled audience all about the apartment they shared, the classes they were taking, and the new people they had met.

Katy then told the Pratts about her first few months at the state college in Elmsford. She also entertained them with hilarious tales of the ups and downs of working in the Children's Department at Marbury's—making her tales all the more enjoyable by dividing up her cache of lollipops, giving each of the twins one for now and four to treat themselves to later. All in all, Katy reported, she was having a wonderful time, juggling her busy schedule, pursuing wholeheartedly the things that were important to her, and making new friends at each and every one of the endeavors she undertook.

"It sounds as if you're having a great time at State," Chris finally said, leading the way down Old Woods Road, a street known for the large tumbledown Victorian houses on it, most of them the homes of some of the town's oldest citizens. "Do you ever see any of our other friends from Whittington High around the campus? I know several of the kids we graduated with are going there. Let's see, there's Holly Anderson and Beth Thompson, of course.'' Chris mentioned the names of the twins' very best friends from their high-school days. ''We'll have to give them both a call as soon as we get back, Sooz. And then there's B. J. Wilkins. Who else?''

Katy wrinkled up her nose. ''Don't forget Felicia Harris.''

Chris groaned at the mere mention of the familiar name. Felicia Harris was pretty, extremely popular with a certain crowd at school, and one of the snobbiest, most conceited people any of the three of them had ever met. She also happened to be the daughter of Whittington's mayor, a fact she rarely let people forget.

As if her own tendencies toward selfishness weren't enough, Felicia also held a sort of grudge against the Pratt twins. That had begun a year and a half earlier during *The Hot Fudge Sunday Affair*, the time when Chris has been selected to play an honorary role in the celebration of the town's one-hundred-year anniversary. It was a great honor—one that Chris truly deserved—but one that Felicia thought would be more fitting for the daughter of the town's mayor. During Whittington's week-long celebration, Felicia had tried her hardest to get Chris and Susan in trouble because of a secret charade they were attempting in the midst of all the festivities. She would have succeeded, too, if it hadn't turned out that a century earlier, the town's founders had shared a devilish little secret of their own.

"And how is Felicia?" Susan asked politely. She was, after all, the type of person who never liked to say a negative word about anybody. "I hope she's enjoying college life."

"She's the same as always, I'm afraid," Katy replied. "Of course, she didn't even want to go to State. The whole thing was her father's idea. She wanted to go to some fancy college where she could major in horseback riding, but her father insisted on State.

"She refuses to try to fit in. She dresses up for classes as if she were gong to a party, when just about everybody else wears jeans. She just joined the most exclusive sorority on campus, Alpha Beta Alpha, and now she acts as if the only people good enough for her to talk to are the other members. Then there's her new boyfriend. She acts as if he's Mr. Perfect."

"Is he a student at State, too?" asked Chris.

Katy shook her head. "No. As Felicia put it the last time I overheard her bragging, she finds college boys 'too immature.' She claims she's ready to go out with an older man."

"Older?" Susan was surprised. "How much older?"

"I'm not sure, but I think he's twenty-three."

"Gosh," said Chris. "And Felicia is barely eighteen."

"At least he's not as old as Mr. Krigley," Katy said with a giggle.

The three girls were just riding by the house that belonged to one of the town's best-known—and least seen—citizens. "Old Mr. Krigley," as he was commonly called, was said to be in his eighties. Yet he rarely, if ever, left his house, a ramshackle old Victorian at the very end of Old Woods Road that was so run-down it looked as if it were haunted. People in Whittington called him a hermit because he was never seen around town. To the Pratts and all the other girls and boys who had grown up in that town, he had always been a rather mysterious, even frightening, figure.

"Well, that boyfriend of Felicia's might as well be as old as Mr. Krigley," Chris teased back. "At any rate, you're right, Katy. It does sound as if good old Felicia hasn't changed a bit. But enough about her. Tell us all about what's going to happen over Homecoming Weekend. After all, your younger sister is the chairperson. She's a senior now, isn't she?"

"That's right, she is. Kelly is also the president of the senior class," Katy said proudly. "Right now, she's trying to come up with an idea for the senior class project. You know, the big event that starts right after Christmas break, when all the kids in the senior class pitch in and volunteer to do something to help the community. She wants to do something really special this year, but unfortunately she hasn't been able to come up with a thing. I keep telling her not to worry, that she'll think up something wonderful after Homecoming Weekend is over."

"I'm sure she'll get inspired, once all the excitement and planning for this weekend is over," said Chris. "But tell us about what's going on this weekend."

"Let's see. Tonight is the opening of the Autumn Harvest Festival, of course. And then, tomorrow morning, there's the pancake breakfast over at the community center. In the afternoon there's the big Homecoming game. That will be one of the real highlights of the weekend. After all, Whittington is playing Elmsford, their all-time rival.''

She went on to describe the rest of the events, ending with the Homecoming dance at the high-school gym Sunday evening. Meanwhile, the girls turned their bikes around and, still enjoying their lollipops, started heading back toward the Pratts' house.

Suddenly Katy slapped her forehead. ''Oh, my gosh! I almost forgot. And this is the best part!''

''What is it?'' asked Susan.

''We're all going to be on TV!''

''On television? Really? Katy, what are you talking about?'' Chris demanded excitedly.

Katy went on to explain that the local television station, WIT-TV, was going to be featuring live coverage of the events of Whittington High School's Homecoming all weekend, as they happened. The special short features would be interspersed with the regular programming, popping up between the newscasts and other shows that were aired on the station regularly.

''Gosh,'' Chris said, her brown eyes shining brightly. ''TV! That's fantastic!''

She sighed. ''Boy, what a weekend this is going to be. Dances, parties, football games, a harvest fair . . . and as if that weren't enough, now we find out we're all going to be on television. I can tell that this is going to turn out to be one of the most exciting and most memorable weekends of my entire life!''

As she spoke, Chris had no idea how true her words would turn out to be. Or that the fair, parties, dances, football games, and even the fact that all the events of the weekend would be televised were only going to be part of it.

Two

The Whittington town park, a long, narrow stretch of grass right smack in the middle of town, was brimming with activity by the time the Pratt twins arrived, just before eight o'clock. The Autumn Harvest Festival was already well under way, and the crowds, the loud music, and the strings of white lights everywhere promised to make it one of the most exciting fairs the girls had ever attended. While it was a cool November evening, the electricity in the air, the number of people at the park, and the heavy sweaters and wool clothing that everyone had had the foresight to wear all kept the fair goers from becoming uncomfortable.

Three long aisles, already packed, had been created by the dozens of booths that had been set up in time for tonight's opening. Many of the booths housed games of chance and games of skill, offering large stuffed animals as prizes. Others contained displays by local businesses. And the rest offered for sale every kind of food imaginable, from hot dogs to cotton candy to homemade fudge.

There were large tents further back, in which organizations like the 4-H Club, the Girl Scouts and Boy Scouts, and the Lions Club sponsored exhibits of quilts, machinery, and prize-winning jams and jellies. All the schools in the area had donated paintings for the art exhibit; in past years, Susan had always had at least one of her pieces included there. There were also rides set up in the very back: a roller coaster, a Ferris wheel, even a long, curving slide. And in the middle of it all was a bandstand lit up by lights and decorated with orange and brown streamers and balloons, at the moment serving as the stage for a local rock band. In fact, the area right around it had been left clear for dancing, and many couples had already given in to the irresistible beat and started doing exactly that.

The Pratt twins were breathless as they surveyed this scene, anticipating an evening of fun. They would not only have their usual good time at one of Whittington's most enjoyable annual events but, because this was the beginning of Homecoming Weekend, they also would be bound to meet up with old friends, and to chat and catch up on all the news.

"Gee, this is exciting," said Chris, already tapping her foot to the beat of the rock band whose sound was pulsing throughout the park. "I bet we'll run into just about everybody we know here tonight." She looked around, eagerly searching for a familiar face.

"I hope we see some of our old teachers," Susan remarked, also scanning the faces. "I'd really like the chance to tell Mr. Smith, my art teacher from both my junior and senior years, all about the classes I'm taking at Morgan. I'm sure he'd be interested. Do you see him anywhere, Chris? Chris? *Chris?*"

But Chris wasn't paying attention. She was too busy ogling the cameras and wires and lights that were being hauled in through the clearing between the booth selling hot mulled cider and the booth promising oversized stuffed teddy bears to anyone able to toss three out of four balls into a hoop. From what she could tell, the film crew from the local television station, WIT-TV, had just arrived and was about to begin setting up for their live broadcast.

"Look, Sooz!" she cried, grabbing her twin's arm and jumping up and down. "It's the TV people! Oooh, I don't think I really believed until this moment that we were actually going to be on television."

"Not so fast," Susan warned, laughing. "The TV people are here to film the events of this Homecoming Weekend, Chris, not to turn you into a celebrity! Look around you. There are hundreds of people here. The chances of you—or any particular person, for that matter—being singled out are pretty slim."

"I know." Chris's excitement had cooled down, but not completely. "But maybe they'll want to interview some of the people here at the fair tonight. Talk to them a little bit, find out how they're enjoying themselves at the first event of Homecoming Weekend, that kind of thing. In that case, I'd say that I have as good a chance as anybody. By the way, how do I look? Just in case, I mean."

Susan surveyed her twin sister carefully. She had to

admit that tonight Chris looked as if she could indeed be a television celebrity. She was wearing black pants and a baggy wool sweater with jade green and purple stripes, two bright colors that the more outgoing Pratt twin always enjoyed wearing. Her shoulder-length chestnut brown hair was loose, decorated with a large clip in the exact same colors as the sweater.

Susan couldn't help comparing the eye-catching outfit her sister was wearing to the more subdued outfit she had chosen. She had on a bulky white turtleneck, hand-knit by her grandmother, and her hair was pulled back into a ponytail and fastened with a tortoiseshell barrette. She was amused by the contrast, thinking about just how different she and her sister really were, even though their faces happened to be the mirror image of each other.

"Well, Chris, you do look nice enough to be on television. But that's not why we're here, remember? We're here to enjoy the fair . . . and to see as many of our old friends from high school as we can. And that's exactly what I intend to do."

The words were barely out of her mouth when she felt someone tap her on the shoulder. She whirled around and found Beth Thompson, her very best friend from high school, standing at her side.

"Susan!" she cried. "I'm so glad to see you!"

"Me, too, Beth. And you look wonderful!"

Beth did look pretty tonight. The shy girl with the dark curly hair looked as if she had grown up quite a bit since starting her freshman year at State. But underneath her shorter hairstyle, her new outfit, and an air of increased self-confidence, she was still the same old Beth. And Susan couldn't have been more delighted.

The two girls immediately began chatting together calmly—quite a contrast to Chris, who had just run into Holly Anderson, her best friend since elementary school.

"Holly!" Chris shrieked. "You got your hair cut! Oooh, I love it. It looks great. Where'd you get it cut?"

Chris and her tall, blond friend launched into a loud, animated discussion of their social lives, their new schools, and the classes they were taking. The four girls were so busy talking, in fact, that they didn't even notice when a boy about their age approached their group, moving hesitantly as if he didn't know whether or not he'd be welcome.

"Excuse me," he finally said, looking at Susan, "but aren't you Susan Pratt?"

"Why, yes, I am," Susan replied, a little bit surprised. "Do I know you?"

"Sort of." The boy grinned. "You and I used to work on the school newspaper together, back when we were sophomores. We both tried out for the sophomore class editor . . . and you won. I was so crushed that I left the newspaper and went out for the debating team instead."

Susan laughed. "Yes, now I remember. You're Adam Leeds, aren't you?

"That's right. It's nice to see you again."

"You, too, Adam. What are you doing now?"

"I'm a freshman at Tyler University, majoring in

English . . . and I just joined the debating team. Listen, I'd really love to talk to you, but I was just heading over to the Civic Association's booth to get some hot chocolate for Ms. Carpenter, who was my English teacher during my junior year. I ran into her over by the bandstand. Speaking of the bandstand, how about a dance a little later on?'' He flashed that same grin once again, ''Just because you and I were in competition with each other once doesn't mean it has to be like that forever.''

Susan was blushing by the time he moved on. But she quickly resumed her conversation with Beth, and before long all four girls were chattering away once again.

The small group of friends pledged to stick together for the rest of the evening. They were anxious to catch up on all the news of the past three months, and now that they were together, they didn't want to be separated. They wandered around the fair, talking away, sampling some of the food, stopping to interrupt their conversation only when they ran into another one of their acquaintances from high-school days.

Much to their delight, just about everyone they knew seemed to be at the Harvest Festival. Many of their friends, and casual acquaintances as well, joined them to reminisce about their days together in high school and fill one another in on what they were doing now.

And Susan did finally find Mr. Smith. She spent a good ten minutes talking his ear off, telling him all about her courses at Morgan. He, in turn, was pleased

that his star pupil was enjoying art school so much—
and, from the way it sounded, doing extremely well
there.

The evening was as much fun as it had promised to
be. Chris, however, was getting a little restless by the
time the members of the rock band announced over the
park's loudspeaker system that they were taking a short
break before beginning their second set. In the meantime, a disk jockey from the local radio station would
be playing records so that the couples who were gath-
ered near the bandstand, not far from where the twins
and their friends were talking, could keep on dancing.

When one of Chris's favorite songs came on, she
found herself unable to resist the urge to start moving
around herself.

"Chris, what are you *doing*?" Holly pretended to
scold.

"Well, I can't help it," Chris returned. "I just feel
like dancing, that's all. And I'm going to dance,
whether there's anyone around to dance with or not."

"I'll volunteer for the job," said a good-looking
boy with shaggy blond hair. He seemed to have appeared from out of nowhere.

"Do I know you?" Chris asked, blinking. He did
look a little bit familiar, but she couldn't quite place
him.

"No, but I know you. At least, I've been watching
you for the last half hour."

"Watching me?"

"From the bandstand. I'm in the group you've been
listening to all evening. That is, I hope you've been
listening. I play the bass guitar."

Suddenly it all made sense. That was why he looked familiar. "That's right, you are." Chris was pleased at having been singled out. "Well, then," she said flirtatiously, "let's see if you can dance as well as you can play the bass guitar! By the way, my name is Chris."

"And I'm Todd," said the bassist. "Now how about showing these kids what dancing is all about?"

Chris and Todd danced well together—so well that they kept on dancing when the first number ended. In fact, they were about to begin their fourth dance when they suddenly noticed that right next to the bandstand, something—or someone—was causing a great commotion.

"One thing is for sure," Holly commented, looking over in the direction of all the activity. "That girl does know how to make an entrance."

And her statement was certainly true. Standing a few hundred feet away from the bandstand was Felicia Harris, the mayor's daughter, looking as if she had just stepped off the pages of a fashion magazine. She posed dramatically for a few seconds, then pranced across the green, her head held high, pausing every once in a while to give an arrogant toss of her head.

The outfit she was wearing perfectly complemented her stance. She had on a black jumpsuit made of stretchy fabric, accessorized with brilliant jewelry. Her waist-length blond hair was fastened at one side with a rhinestone barrette. On her feet were black shoes with heels so high it was amazing that she could even walk, especially on the rough ground here at the park.

Most noticeable, however, was the smug look on her face. And the reason for her expression was as apparent as the glint in her eyes and the self-satisfied smile on her lips. On her arm was an extremely good-looking young man. He was tall and dark and had an easy smile. In fact, every time he smiled, he flashed two rows of perfect teeth that were as bright as those of a model in a toothpaste commercial.

"Uh, oh. Here she comes," Holly said, rolling her eyes. "Gosh, from the way Felicia is strutting around, you'd think *she* was running for Homecoming queen this weekend along with those six girls from the senior class."

"Well, you have to admit that she does look pretty," Susan said, wanting to be kind.

Holly glanced over in the direction of all the commotion once again. "She does look nice, I guess . . . but wow! Check out the guy she's with. He's really cute."

Whatever their feelings about Felicia, all four girls had to admit that her boyfriend was, indeed, good-looking. And from the reaction of the people around him, it seemed as if he were also quite charming. The crowd around the bandstand parted to let the attractive couple pass through, the murmurs making it clear that everyone was just as impressed as the twins and their friends.

And then Felicia happened to glance over in their direction. When she spotted Susan and Chris, the two girls she thought of as her rivals, a look of real determination crossed her face. She tugged gently on her boyfriend's arm and whispered something in his ear.

Then she headed toward the foursome, her attentive date close at her side.

"It looks as if we're going to get to meet Felicia's new friend," Chris observed.

"Right," Holly agreed. "Whether we want to or not."

"Why, if it isn't Christine and Susan, the famous Pratt twins," cooed Felicia, sashaying over to the little group, her chin held high. She tossed her head for effect. "How lovely to see you again. You, too, Beth. Hi, Holly."

"Hello, Felicia," said Susan, the only one who could manage to sound sincere. "It's nice to see you, too."

"Clark, I'd like you to meet some of my friends from here in town," Felicia went on. "Some dear, sweet girls that I've know for *such* a long time."

She introduced each one of them, then said in a triumphant voice, "And this, girls, is Clarkson P. Rutherford III. But you can call him Clark." She giggled, then added, "Just like I do."

Chris and Susan exchanged amused looks.

"We're pleased to meet you, Clark," said Susan.

"Gee, Clark, I certainly hope you're not bored tonight," Chris couldn't resist saying. "The fair is great, but everyone here seems much more interested in talking to their old friends. And Felicia didn't even go to school here in Whittington; she was always away at that boarding school she went to. Unless, of course, *you* went to Whittington High School."

Clark cleared his throat, then flashed a big smile. "No, as a matter of fact, I'm not from around here."

"Clark went to high school at the Oxford Prep School for Boys," Felicia said loftily. "Surely you've heard of it."

"Oh, of course," Chris said in an equally lofty tone. "Goodness, hasn't everyone?"

"No, I didn't go to school around here," Clark went on, "but even so, I've been looking forward to this Homecoming Weekend for a long time. For one thing, Felicia is her sorority's representative at the Civic Association's pancake breakfast tomorrow. She's in charge of fund-raising for the new town playground."

He smiled at her proudly. "But the real high point, of course, is tonight, right here at the fair." He put his arm around Felicia and flashed his smile once again.

"What do you mean?" asked Beth.

"Yes, what's so special about tonight in particular?" Holly wanted to know.

"Oh, haven't you heard?" Felicia tossed her head so that her rhinestone barrette glistened. "My father is giving a speech tonight. As a way of getting the Homecoming festivities under way and all."

"That's right," said Clark. "Mayor Harris's welcoming address promises to be the highlight of the evening."

Chris was about to make a comment about Clark's claim, ignoring her sister's warning glance. But before she had a chance, Felicia spoke.

"The television people certainly expect my father's speech to be the highlight," she said, glancing over at the people from WIT-TV. "They're planning to broadcast every word of it."

Sure enough, when the four girls looked over at the impressive collection of cameras and sound equipment and special lightning, they saw that the film crew had indeed set up around the bandstand, no doubt the place from which Mayor Harris would be making his speech.

"Yes, Mayor Harris will be getting a lot of publicity out of this," Clark observed.

"That's right, he will," Felicia agreed. "And that's especially important because he'll be running for re-election next November. Of course, I plan to do my part tomorrow, when the most thrilling thing is going to happen—"

But Clark's enthusiasm caused him to cut her off before she had a chance to finish. "The mayor's speech is going to be great, too," he was saying. Turning to the twins, he explained, "Tonight he's going to come out really strongly against the proposed development of the land out near Old Woods Road."

"Wait a minute," Susan demanded. "What do you mean, the proposed development of the land out near Old Woods Road? *What* development?"

"Oh, it's a plan somebody came up with a few months ago. It would involve knocking down those dilapidated old houses out on Old Woods Road and turning that whole run-down area into a shopping center."

"What dilapidated old houses?" Chris was trying desperately to make some sense out of what he was saying. Suddenly it clicked, and she snapped her fingers. "Oh, I know. You mean like old Mr. Krigley's place?"

"That's one of the houses that would be affected.

The way the plan would work is that old Mr. Krigley and all the other residents of Old Woods Road would receive a lot of money from the land development company for those tumbledown houses of theirs— probably more money than they'd ever get from an individual buyer. I must say, it would probably be the best thing that ever happened to those old folks living over there. And the land developers, meanwhile, would then be free to convert that land into some really useful space. A shopping center, in fact.''

''You're leaving out the most important detail,'' Felicia said, sounding annoyed. ''My father happens to be very much against that plan. He's simply not interested in adding another shopping center to Whittington.''

''That's right,'' Clark was quick to agree. ''And I'm one hundred percent behind him, too.''

''Oh, I know you are, Clarkie, sweetie,'' Felicia cooed, grasping his arm tightly. ''And I know you're going to do your best to help Daddy win when election time come around.''

Turning back to the girls, she said proudly, ''Clark is one of Daddy's most loyal supporters. He works in City Hall as one of Daddy's assistants. As a matter of fact, his office is right down the hall from the mayor's office, isn't it, Clark, honey?''

She winked at Chris, then said, ''Oooh, isn't he just the most wonderful thing you've ever seen in your *life*?''

Before Chris or one of the others had a chance to get in their two cents about Clarkson P. Rutherford III, there was a second commotion over by the bandstand. Mayor Harris had just appeared, surrounded by three of his other assistants. A cameraman was already filming his arrival, which, the girls knew, was being broadcast live.

"Oh, look. Here's Daddy now. Right on time, as usual. It's nine-twenty-nine, and his speech is scheduled for nine-thirty. I just love a man who's prompt, don't you? Come on, Clark, let's try to get closer so we can hear better."

"Did you *hear* her?" Beth whispered after Felicia had trotted off with Clark in tow. " 'Certainly, Clarkie, dear.' 'Whatever you say, Clarkie, honey.' Oh, yuck. She's unbelievable, that Felicia."

"Well, maybe she's just so crazy about that new boyfriend of hers that she doesn't realize how silly she's acting," Susan said.

"Oh, Susan you're so kind and patient, always giving everybody the benefit of the doubt," said Holly.

"Let's move closer to the bandstand," Chris suggested. She craned her neck over the crowd and saw that the mayor was getting ready to make his speech. "That way, we'll be able to hear Mayor Harris more easily."

The twins and their friends began moving toward the bandstand. While they all continued chattering away, Susan had her eyes glued to the mayor. She hadn't been paying very close attention to him at first; in fact, she was merely keeping an eye on him to see if he were ready to start his speech. But she suddenly noticed a change in his posture.

"And I understand that the dance on Sunday night is going to be really terrific," Holly was saying to the others.

But Susan wasn't really listening. She was too absorbed in watching Mayor Harris. From what she could tell, he had just opened up a folded piece of paper, no doubt his notes for his speech, and a smaller piece of paper had slipped out. It was reading that note, or whatever it was, that was causing such an extreme reaction in the mayor and the other people around him.

"Chris, look," she said, grabbing her sister's arm. "Look at Mayor Harris, up on the bandstand. There's something strange going on up there."

Her twin stopped her conversation midsentence to see what it was that her sister was so excited about. Sure enough, Mayor Harris was talking in hushed tones to his three assistants. It didn't take long for Clark, another one of his assistants, to hop up onto the bandstand to join them. Soon all five people were talking together seriously—and all five looked worried.

Then Clark took the microphone. His handsome face was creased with concern as he began to speak.

"Ladies and gentlemen," he said, "may I please have your attention for a few moments. I have a special announcement to make, and I'm afraid it's some rather bad news. Mayor Harris will not be giving his speech tonight."

A surprised murmur rose up from the crowd. Clark held up his hands for silence.

"As difficult as it is to believe," he went on, speaking slowly, "someone has sent the mayor a threatening note. He has been advised to postpone his speech indefinitely, and he agrees that that is the best course of action to follow. Tonight's festivities will continue as planned, but Mayor Harris will be leaving immediately to meet with the chief of the Whittington Police Department.''

There was a flurry of excitement as the mayor and his assistants filed off the stage and headed away. All of this, meanwhile, was being broadcast live by WIT-TV's camera crew.

"Gosh, a threatening note," Susan said once the records had begun playing again, the disk jockey having no doubt been instructed to change the tone of the fair back to one of merriment as quickly as possible. "What a terrible thing!"

"It's difficult to believe that something like that could happen here in Whittington," Chris agreed. "Especially to someone as well liked as Mayor Harris."

"It's true that he's a popular mayor," Susan said thoughtfully. "Goodness, who could possibly want to do such an awful thing?"

"I, for one, have no idea," Chris said, suddenly sounding a bit impatient. "But here comes Todd, looking as if he's ready for another round on the dance floor. I intend to forget all about politics for now and spend the rest of the night having a good time."

With that, she was off. Her twin, meanwhile, remained pensive, still very much absorbed by the evening's disturbing turn of events.

And then, a minute or two later, Adam Leeds reappeared.

"Well, Susan," he said with a grin, "I'm free for that dance now. That is, if you're still interested."

She was, and it didn't take long before she, too, forgot all about the mysterious threatening note that the town's mayor had just received.

Three

Chris was lying in her bed, inhaling the delicious smell of freshly brewed coffee and toasted English muffins, thinking about heading downstairs for breakfast. For the moment, however, she was enjoying lingering beneath the blue flower-sprigged comforter, her head cradled by downy pillows, wiggling her toes under the crisp blue sheets.

There was nothing like the relaxed feeling of being back at home, in her own room, surrounded by all her things: the swimming trophy she had won during her senior year of high school, her favorite books, several paintings done by her sister displayed on her walls. And early on a Saturday morning, when she didn't have a care in the world, seemed like the perfect time to appreciate the first day of vacation she had had in months.

She felt as if she could lie there forever, basking in

the bright November sunlight that was shining through
the window. She turned over and pulled the covers up
to her chin. And then, just as she was wondering
whether or not she felt like going back to sleep, there
was a soft but determined knock on the door.

"Go away," Chris called, pulling the covers over
her head. In a muffled voice, she added, "I'm on
vacation."

The knock came a second time.

"Chris, it's me, Susan," her twin said through the
door. "I have something important to talk to you
about."

"Unless it has something to do with breakfast, I
don't want to hear it," said Chris. But finally she
poked her head out from underneath the covers. "All
right. Come on in, Sooz."

Her twin, she discovered, was not only already
dressed, wearing a pair of brown wool pants and a
beige sweater, but she had an alert look in her eye that
let Chris know immediately that it was not breakfast
that she was so anxious to talk about. Tucked under
her arm was a newspaper.

"This had better be good, Sooz." Chris sat up in
bed. By now she, too, was fully awake.

"It's *not* good," Susan replied, her expression troubled. "That's the whole point."

With that she held up the newspaper she had brought
in so that her sister could read the headlines.

"Sooz, what's this all about?" Chris mumbled. In
order to answer her own question, she quickly read the
front page of the Whittington *Herald*.

MAYOR HARRIS FALTERS! the headline read.

Right below was a photograph of the mayor. In it, he was looking down at a small square of paper. The expression on his face was one of fear.

"Wait a second," Chris said, grabbing the newspaper away from Susan. "Let me see that."

Quickly she skimmed the front-page article of the *Herald*. The facts reported were certainly accurate enough. It said that the night before, Mayor Harris had been scheduled to give a speech at the Homecoming Weekend's kickoff event, the opening of the town's annual Autumn Harvest Festival. It told of the threatening note he had received, and how he had cancelled his speech at the last minute.

Instead of sounding sympathetic, however, the tone of the article was accusatory. Rather than showing Mayor Harris as the victim of a terrible occurrence, the article portrayed him as the one at fault by refusing to go ahead with his speech.

"I can't believe this!" Chris cried. "Why, this article isn't fair to poor Mayor Harris at all."

"I know," Susan said softly, sitting down on the edge of her sister's bed. "And wait, there's more." She turned the newspaper to the editorial page, pointing out a short piece written by the editor of the paper.

"In this editorial, it says that Mayor Harris acted wrongly, claiming that he should have gone ahead and given his speech anyway. It says that to give in—to cancel the speech—was letting whoever sent that note win."

Susan sighed. "No matter what the tone of the

newspaper, the people of Whittington are apparently up in arms. While you were catching up on your beauty sleep, I was out talking to some of our neighbors. People are outraged by what happened. They intend to get to the bottom of this—and fast. They want to find out who's responsible for that threatening note and make sure that person is arrested as soon as possible.''

"Wow," Chris said breathlessly. "This whole thing is really turning into a big deal, isn't it?"

"Poor Felicia," Susan said all of a sudden. "If I were in her shoes, I know I'd be feeling terrible right now."

"Poor *Felicia*!" Chris returned. "What are you talking about, Sooz? She's probably so wrapped up in her new boyfriend—that . . . that *Clark* person—that she's not even aware of what's going on with her father. It's Mayor Harris whom *I'm* worried about. He's the one who must be feeling awful. He's such a nice man, too. Remember how kind he was to us at the end of Centennial Week, when he accidentally found out about our little scheme?"

Chris thought for a few seconds, then said, "Gee, I almost feel like hopping on my bicycle right now and going over to his house to talk to him about all this."

Susan immediately brightened. "I was hoping you'd say that, Chris, because it just so happens that that's exactly what I had in mind!"

"What?" Chris blinked in confusion. "Are you really serious, Sooz? Wait a minute. Maybe I'm just dreaming. Maybe I'm not awake yet—"

"Oh, you're awake. And you're about to do precisely what you just suggested.'' With that, Susan began to drag her sister out of bed.

"Sooz, what about *breakfast*?" Chris cried. "Surely you don't expect me to spend my vacation running around Whittington, sticking my nose into other people's problems—where it doesn't especially *belong*, mind you—without even stopping for breakfast?"

"You can grab a piece of toast on the way out,'' Susan replied calmly. "Right now, you and I are going to talk to Mayor Harris. The man is in a tight spot, and he needs help. And who could possibly be more qualified than we are to help someone who's in trouble?"

Even Chris had to admit that her twin had a point.

"Well, Sooz, do you have any great ideas about what we're going to say to him?" Chris was asking half an hour later as she and her sister stood on the front steps of Mayor Harris's house, waiting for someone to answer the doorbell. It was a big white house, the largest and most impressive in Whittington. "Maybe you had something like this in mind: 'Hi, Mayor Harris. We heard that someone sent you a threatening note last night, and we're so nosy that we just couldn't resist stopping by to ask you how that makes you feel.' "

"No, of course not,'' Susan replied matter-of-factly. "We're going to pretend that we're here to visit his daughter.''

"Us, visiting Felicia?" Chris cried. "That's the craziest thing I've ever heard in my entire life!"

"Yes, of course it is. But Mayor Harris doesn't know that.''

"Okay, then. Since you seem to have thought this whole thing out already, what are we gong to say to Felicia when she comes downstairs in her nightgown, wondering what on earth the Pratt twins, of all people, are doing paying her a visit . . . so early on a Saturday morning, no less?"

"Nothing. Because Felicia isn't home."

Chris cast her sister a skeptical glance. "And how can you be so sure of that?"

"First of all," Susan said in her usual logical manner, "look around and you'll see that her car is gone."

Chris did. Sure enough, Felicia's bright red sports car, her graduation gift from her father, was nowhere to be seen. "Maybe it's parked in the garage," she suggested.

"It's not, I can assure you. That's because, second of all, this morning is the Civic Association's pancake breakfast."

"So?"

"So I'm sure she's already over at the Community Center, acting the part of the perfect hostess. Don't you remember Clark mentioning that Felicia is her sorority's representative at that event? He said something about raising funds for a new playground."

Chris grinned. "Boy, I'm impressed. I can see what makes you such a sharp investigator."

Susan was cautious, however. "We'll see. After all, we still don't know how much we're going to find out from our little visit—that is, if we find out anything at all."

Much to the twins' surprise, when the front door was finally answered it wasn't Mayor Harris who opened it. Instead it was opened by a man in a suit, someone whom they didn't recognize.

He eyed them suspiciously, then asked, "Can I help you girls?"

Susan, as usual, was prepared for anything. "Good morning. I'm Susan Pratt, and this is my sister Chris. We're here to see Felicia."

"Felicia's not here right now," the man replied gruffly. "Come back another time."

Much to the girls' dismay, he started to shut the door in their faces. But before he had a chance to close them out completely, they heard another voice from inside the house call, "It's all right. They're just friends of Felicia's. Let them in."

The man frowned. Then, with a grunt that indicated he didn't really think it was a good idea at all, he slowly opened the front door to let the girls pass through.

Right inside, in the living room, Mayor Harris was sitting on the couch, looking troubled. A cup of coffee was on the table next to him, along with that morning's *Herald*. His expression brightened as they walked in, as if he were genuinely pleased to see them.

"Come on in, girls. Have a seat." To the man in the suit, he said, "It's all right, really. I know these girls."

After the man stepped away, retreating to some other part of the house, Mayor Harris explained, "Sorry about all that, Susan and Chris. He's from the police department." He shook his head slowly and added, "Ever since I got that threatening note last night, the police have had the house under constant surveillance. Do you believe that I actually have body-guards?''

"I understand completely," Susan said. "I'm sure the police are very concerned. And you must be extremely upset, Mayor Harris."

"Oh, I am. Of course I am." He frowned. "I can't imagine who would threaten me. It's such an . . . *extreme* thing to do. Why, if someone disagrees with my policies, there are all kinds of channels to pursue. But to come out and actually *threaten* me . . .''

It was obvious that the man was beside himself with despair. The girls' hearts went out to him. Chris was certain that this was a bad time to be visiting . . . and especially to be pretending to be looking for Felicia. She was feeling a little uncomfortable and was on the verge of suggesting that they go.

So she was very surprised when she heard her sister say in that gentle voice of hers, "Mayor Harris, do you think Chris and I could possibly have a look at that note?"

"Susan!" Chris cried.

But already Mayor Harris was nodding.

"I don't see why not," he said. "It's not as if what it says is any great secret or anything. Why, I'm sure that by now this entire town is buzzing about it." With his chin he gestured toward the newspaper lying on the table.

"It's over there on the desk, girls. Feel free to take a look at it. But don't touch it. Fingerprints and all."

"Of course," Susan said.

She and Chris went over and looked at the note. The

words were made from letters that had been cut out of magazines and then glued to an ordinary sheet of white paper. They spelled out, DON'T GIVE YOUR SPEECH TONIGHT OR YOU'LL BE SORRY! I MEAN BUSINESS!

"Gee, that's terrible," Susan said. "I wish there were something we could do to help."

Mayor Harris smiled. "Thank you. It's very nice of you girls to be so concerned. But the police are working on this around the clock, and I'm sure they'll catch the culprit soon enough.

"By the way," the mayor continued, "I'm afraid that the police detective was right. Felicia isn't here right now. She's over at the pancake breakfast. Shall I tell her you stopped by?"

"Oh, no, that's all right," Susan was quick to reply. "We'll see her later on this morning. We plan to go over to the pancake breakfast ourselves." She started moving toward the door. "Well, I guess we'd better be going now. 'Bye, Mayor Harris."

Chris couldn't wait to get out. But as she and her sister walked silently out the door, back toward the bicycles they had left leaning against a tree right outside the mayor's house, she noticed an unmistakable glint in Susan's eyes. She had seen that look before, more than once. And if she knew anything about her twin at all, she knew for sure that Susan wasn't about to walk away from this mystery that had so suddenly and so unexpectedly fallen upon the girls' hometown of Whittington.

Once the girls were back on their bicycles, Susan was silent for a long time. Chris knew that her twin sister's mind was clicking away, but at the moment, she was more concerned with the fact that she was hungry. After all, she had left the house that morning with nothing more for breakfast than a single piece of toast. She scrounged around in her jacket pocket, feeling for something to eat. She came up with two lollipops, left over from the twins' biking expedition with Katy the day before.

Once her hunger was starting to be satisfied with the yellow one, she found she could stand her twin sister's silence no longer.

"All right, Sooz. What is it?"

"Hmmm? Oh, I was just thinking, that's all."

"I can *see* that you were thinking," Chris replied impatiently, sucking on her lemon lollipop. "What I want to know is what you were thinking about."

"Why, Mayor Harris, of course."

"I should have guessed," Chris groaned. "Sooz, you may have forgotten, but this weekend is *supposed* to be a vacation for us. I—"

But Susan wasn't interested in listening to excuses. "I was thinking about the fact that we have simply got to help him. Mayor Harris, I mean. I was trying to decide what we should do next."

"Susan Pratt!" Chris squeezed her hand brakes, and her bicycle screeched to a halt. "You can't be serious! Surely you don't expect that you and I are going to spend our Homecoming Weekend investigating some . . . some *crazy* person who's sending threatening notes made out of letters cut from a magazine to our town's mayor. Surely you don't expect that I'm going to get involved in something that the police are already looking into, something that could turn out to be really dangerous. . . ."

Susan, too, had stopped her bicycle, but much less dramatically. She was about five feet ahead of her sister, and she looked over her shoulder as she patiently replied, "Surely you don't expect me to do it all by myself."

Chris's mouth just dropped open. Quickly she snapped it shut.

"It sounds to me as if you've already made up your mind about this."

"Oh, I have. Chris, you and I have no choice but to help find out who sent that awful threatening note to Mayor Harris."

"Really?" Chris said dryly. "And why is that?"

"First, because he helped us during *The Hot Fudge Sunday Affair*, so we owe him a favor. Second, because an important person in our town is in trouble, and we just might be in a better position than the police to help, because we know this town backward and forward and we can get into places that regular police officers and detectives probably can't.

"And third," she went on with a twinkle in her brown eyes, "because you and I can never resist a challenge!"

Chris tried to look grumpy, but in the end she couldn't resist bursting out laughing. "You win," she said with a sigh.

She thought for a few moments, sucking on her lollipop. Then a grin crept slowly across her face. "And I've already come up with the perfect name for this little sleuthing escapade of ours."

"Don't you always?" Susan said with a chuckle. "All right, Chris. What is it this time?"

"Well, this should give you a clue." She held out her lollipop.

"Uh, oh," Susan returned. "Why do I get the feeling that the first word is 'lollipop'?"

"Because you know me so well, that's why," said Chris. "You know me so *very* well, in fact, that you probably won't even be surprised when I tell you that my nickname for this caper we're about to begin is the 'Lollipop Plot.'

The twins were laughing together merrily as they pedaled off.

"Come on, Chris, follow me. I've already decided what our first step should be." Susan turned off the road they were on, as if she were heading for a short cut.

"Lollipop Plot, here we come," Chris said agreeably, following her sister.

Half to herself, Susan muttered, "Here we come, indeed. I just hope you're feeling brave today!"

Four

"*I don't know about this, Sooz,*" *Chris said uncertainly.* She was standing at the corner of First Street and Clinton, straddling her bicycle, staring up at the imposing three-story brick building surrounded by freshly trimmed shrubs and a large manicured lawn. "Are you absolutely positive this is a good idea?"

"Yes, I'm positive," Susan replied. "Chris, call it intuition if you like, but I can't help thinking that the Old Woods Road development project could well be what's behind that threat against Mayor Harris. After all, in the speech he was scheduled to give he was gong to come out against it. And so looking around City Hall for clues is definitely the obvious way to start."

Chris eyed the building warily. "Even though it's likely that nobody will be in there on a Saturday morning?" she asked nervously.

"*Especially* because there's probably nobody in there," Susan replied confidently. "And not only is it a Saturday morning, either; right about now the Civic Association pancake breakfast should be in full swing. Just about everybody in town should be there. That makes it all the more likely that we'll have this place to ourselves."

Chris was puzzled. "Wait a minute. If nobody is around, then how are we going to get the information we need?"

Susan looked at her and smiled. "Why, by being as sneaky as we possibly can, that's how!"

Once the girls had taken care to hide their bicycles in the lush bushes surrounding city hall, they headed for the front door. Susan confidently lead the way, while Chris followed a few feet behind, looking to the right and to the left to make sure no one saw them. She was fairly certain that no one did; in fact, she was about to let herself relax when she suddenly heard her sister groan.

"Oh, *no!*" cried Susan. She came to a dead halt.

"What is it?" Chris asked anxiously, bumping right into her. In her effort to keep her eyes peeled for possible witnesses, she had neglected to watch where she was going and so she had walked straight into her twin.

Susan was frowning. "This is one problem I hadn't thought of."

"What's *wrong*, Sooz?"

Susan turned to her sister and, looking very disappointed indeed, said, "Chris, the door is locked."

"Oh, is *that* all."

Suddenly Chris was all confidence and bravery, and Susan was the one who was puzzled.

"Wait a minute," Susan said, her eyes growing narrow. "Are you saying that you've already come up with the solution to our problem of being locked out of City Hall?"

"Well, not a solution, exactly . . . Let me put it this way. Since when are the Pratt twins going to let something as simple as a locked door get in their way? Come on, Sooz. You and I just have to try being a little creative, that's all."

Chris remained undaunted even as she and her sister tried every one of the six entrances to the large building, and every single one of them proved to be locked. Susan was about to suggest trying some windows to see if any of them had been left open when she noticed that her twin's expression had suddenly changed.

"What is it, Chris? Have you come up with something?"

"I certainly have. What I've come up with is our ticket inside this place. And there he is."

Susan glanced through the glass window in the side door they had been checking. Inside, halfway down a long corridor, she could see a janitor in a gray uniform carefully mopping the floor.

"Don't say anything for a couple of minutes," Chris instructed, "at least not until we get in."

With that, she began knocking loudly on the door, peering through the window, and looking as miserable as she could. It wasn't long before the janitor noticed her. He came over to the door, opened it up a few inches, and stuck his nose out.

"Hello, there. Is there something I can help you with, young lady?"

"Oh, there certainly is," Chris replied, sounding extremely distressed. "I have to get inside this building right away. It's very important."

The janitor shook his head slowly. "I'm sorry, but this building is closed today."

"But I have to get in. It's . . . it's crucial."

"Sorry, miss."

Suddenly Chris's entire stance changed. With an arrogant toss of her head, she said, "Do you know who I am?"

The janitor began to look uneasy. "Gee, uh, I'm afraid not. You see, I'm new here. I only started this job a couple of weeks ago, and—"

"Then you're not aware that I'm Felicia Harris. You know, Mayor Harris's daughter."

The janitor gulped. "Gee, no. I had no idea."

"Well, I am. This is a friend of mine," Chris went on, gesturing toward Susan. "And my father sent us over to get some very important papers from his office. In fact, I was in such a hurry to pick them up that when I left the house I forgot to bring along the key to the front door of this building. Luckily, I do have the key to his office with me—"

"In that case, come on in, Ms. Harris. Gee, I'm sorry I kept you waiting, but I really didn't know—"

"It's quite all right," Chris assured him in a lofty tone of voice, waving her hand in the air as she strode past him with Susan in tow. "Think nothing of it."

She headed toward the stairs, knowing that the mayor's office was on the second floor of the building, never once looking back.

"Give my regards to your dad," the janitor called after her.

As soon as they reached the top of the stairs and were out of the janitor's earshot, both Susan and Chris burst into uncontrollable giggles.

"Boy, we sure fooled him."

"Chris, you were great. Sometimes I think you should forget all about becoming a lawyer, that you really ought to go into acting."

"At any rate, at least I managed to bluff my way through one more sticky situation."

Once Chris had caught her breath, she said, "Okay, Sooz, we managed to get ourselves into City Hall. And just as you predicted, the building is empty. . . there isn't a soul in sight. But *now* what?"

"I'm afraid we have to sneak back downstairs again. In fact, we have to sneak all the way down to the basement."

"The basement?" Chris blinked. "What's in the basement?"

"Why, that's where all the records are stored, in the Town Archives. Don't you remember that from the tour of City Hall we took in our tenth grade civics class?"

Chris made a funny face. "The only thing I remember about that field trip is that poor Megan Porter sat on my lunch in the bus and had to spend the rest of the day with peanut butter and jelly stains all over her white skirt. Come on, then, Sooz, let's head downstairs.''

Just as the twins had expected, the basement was as quiet and empty as the rest of the building. It was also a little bit eerie. Even so, Susan and Chris didn't waste a moment before getting busy, looking through the file cabinets filled with records in an effort to discover anything they possibly could about the Old Woods Road land development proposal.

It was Susan who tracked down what they needed.

''Here it is,'' she said in a loud whisper after the girls had been looking through the files for ten minutes or so. The one Susan had chosen to peruse was labeled ''Land Sales.'' ''I found exactly what I was looking for.''

''What have you got, Sooz?'' Chris abandoned the file cabinet she had been perusing, carefully glancing through the records inside the top drawer without really knowing what she was looking for but hoping she would recognize something pertinent if she stumbled across it.

''Look at this, Chris,'' Susan said breathlessly, indicating the manila envelope she had opened up and was now sorting through with great interest. ''According to these records, three different plots of land on Old Woods Road have been sold in the past three months. Every one of them is a vacant lot. And every one of them was bought by an organization called the Pearson Corporation.''

Chris looked at her sister and blinked in confusion. ''Gosh, Sooz, what does all that tell us?''

"Plenty. First of all, it tells us that somebody—this Pearson Corporation, whatever that is—is interested in acquiring as much property out on Old Woods Road as it can. Second, they're being fairly secretive about it, at least as far as I know. We'll have to ask Mom and Dad if they've heard anything about this. And third, it tells us that so far no one's sold their house to the Pearson Corporation. Only vacant lots have been purchased. That means that none of the people who are living out there have given up their homes yet."

"But *why*? What does it all mean?"

Susan sighed. "That, I'm afraid, I have yet to figure out." She put the file back together again so that it was exactly the way she had found it, then carefully put the manila folder back in its proper place. "I'm going to need more time. But it is a start, at least."

"Okay, then," Chris said enthusiastically, "so now what?"

"Now," Susan replied, "we get out of here as fast as we can, before anybody finds us snooping around and begins asking questions."

"We'd better sneak back up to the second floor," said Chris. "That way, if we happen to run into the janitor again, he'll think that's where we've been all this time."

"Good thinking, Chris. Come on. Let's head back upstairs."

The girls had no trouble getting up to the second floor without being seen or heard. Once they were up there, Chris opened her mouth, about to start making some noise to keep up the pretense that they had been up there all along, for the janitor's sake. But before she made a single sound, her twin placed a restraining hand on her arm.

"Shhh," Susan said in a soft whisper.

"What is it?" Chris's heart was suddenly pounding.

"I think I hear something. Here, follow me. And keep down."

The girls walked silently, with their knees bent so that no one inside any of the offices would see their silhouettes through the pane of frosted glass inset in each of the doors.

Sure enough, a second or two later Chris knew what her sister had been talking about. From inside one of the offices came the sound of people talking softly. From what the twins could tell, there were two voices, a male voice and a female voice. It sounded as if the two people were arguing. Susan and Chris followed the noise and found that the two people were behind the closed door of Mayor Harris's office.

Wordlessly Susan crept up to the door, taking care to stay down low. She held a warning finger to her lips, but it wasn't necessary. Chris was wide-eyed as she joined her, crouched down outside the door as she, too, listened to the conversation taking place inside the mayor's office.

"Clark, it's bad enough that you asked me to sneak away from the pancake breakfast for a few minutes to meet you here," said the voice that could only belong to Felicia Harris. "And now this. Are you really sure that it's a good idea?"

"Why, of course I am, Felicia," Clark said, his

tone soothing. "Look, I've thought the whole thing out. All you have to do is tell everyone that Mr. Krigley is the person who sent your father that note."

Chris's mouth dropped open. Susan immediately clamped her hand over it as a reminder that this was the worst possible time for the two "spies" to give themselves away.

Chris nodded to show that she understood. Then, wearing an expression of alarm, she mouthed the words, "Mr. Krigley?" Susan just shrugged, looking just as upset and as puzzled as her sister.

"And what makes you so sure that anyone will believe me?" Felicia was saying to Clark on the other side of the closed door.

"You're the mayor's daughter, for goodness sake!" her boyfriend returned. "Of *course* everyone will believe you. Why, you're as respectable as a witness can get. You grew up in this town, you're a freshman at the state college in Elmsford . . . and let's not forget that in addition to all that, you're a nice, down-to-earth, charming, *very* pretty young lady."

Felicia giggled. "Oh, Clark. You're always saying the sweetest things."

"Besides," he went on in a strange voice, "it makes perfect sense that you'd be more anxious than anyone to make sure that the person who sent your father that wretched note be brought to justice."

"But why Mr. Krigley?" Felicia persisted. "Why are you so certain that we should blame him?"

"Felicia, it's crucial that we identify a perpetrator for the crime right away. That way, it'll look as if your father has everything under control. The way he responds to this incident is going to be an important factor in the election next year. Besides, there really is a good chance that Mr. Krigley is the person who sent that note, whether you personally saw him or not.''

''Why do you say that?''

''Because it would be to his benefit for that real estate deal that your father is so much against to go through, that's why.''

''I'm afraid I still don't understand, Clark,'' Felicia said impatiently.

''Look.'' Clark sounded as if he, too, were beginning to get exasperated. ''Old Man Krigley lives in a dilapidated old house on Old Woods Road. Why, that place is practically falling down. It probably should have been condemned years ago. The old man can't help but want to unload a dump like that.

''Then along comes the chance to sell his tumbledown house and his property to some wealthy real-estate developer—somebody who'd pay just about anything to get his land. I'm sure he'd be willing to pay him much more than that old place is worth—and I'm just as sure that Krigley's figured that out by now.''

''Go on,'' Felicia said, still sounding uncertain.

''Okay. So this Mr. Krigley is all set to make a killing on a real estate deal. A real boon, something that just fell from the sky. But there's one hitch: the mayor of this town suddenly comes out *against* the deal. He says it'd be bad for the community, that he wants to preserve the more colorful parts of the town, the sections that represent its history. . . .''

"Don't you think my father is right?" Felicia asked indignantly.

"Sure, sweetie. *I* do. But this old man, Krigley, he's angry, don't you see? He wants to do everything he can to stop your father from preventing this land deal from going ahead.

"So," he finished, "he sends him a threatening note to keep him from making a speech against the deal, one that would be televised and that might actually win some people over to his side. In addition, Krigley probably figures that if the mayor comes out looking bad enough, like somebody who's not strong enough to stand up for what he believes in, no matter what, he might even lose the election next November. And the new mayor, according to his way of thinking, might well turn out to be someone who's in *favor* of the development of Old Woods Road."

"It would be terrible if Daddy lost that election!" Felicia cried. "My father loves being the mayor of this town. It means everything to him. If he lost that position, why, I don't know what it would do to him."

"And what about what it would do to you?" Clark asked in a gentle voice. "You wouldn't be the daughter of the mayor anymore. How do you think your new friends in the Alpha Beta Alpha sorority would feel about that?"

There was a long silence then. The twins just looked at each other—and it was obvious that both of them knew full well that the other was thinking the exact same thing.

"When would you want me to come out and say

that I saw Mr. Krigley pass that note to my father last night?'' Felicia asked.

Clark suddenly sounded very excited. ''This afternoon, when you're interviewed on TV. You're supposed to go to the WIT-TV station at three o'clock today, right?''

''That's right. The TV people thought it would be a nice touch for this feature they're doing on Whittington High School's Homecoming Weekend if they interviewed the daughter of the town's mayor.

''Of course,'' she went on with the haughty tone she used so much of the time, ''they'd probably heard a lot about me already and simply decided that this was the ideal time to put somebody with real star quality on their boring old TV station.''

''I'm sure you're right,'' said Clark. ''So, Felicia, what I'd like you to do—I mean, what I think is the best way you can help fix this terrible situation and set things right again—is to go on TV and tell everyone who's watching that old Mr. Krigley is the one who sent your father that threatening note. I won't be around to coach you, of course, because your father and I have that meeting with the district attorney's office at three, but I know you can handle it.''

There was another long pause, as if Felicia was thinking.

''You make it sound as if Mr. Krigley really is guilty, and that the fact that I didn't actually catch him in the act of threatening my father is just a small detail.''

''That's right, a small detail,'' Clark said enthusiastically. ''A *very* small detail.''

"All right, then, Clark," Felicia said, "While I realize that I wouldn't exactly be telling the truth if I went on TV and said that I saw Mr. Krigley put that threatening note in my father's folder at the fair last night, I do believe that you're only trying to do what's best for my father, for the town . . . and for me. And so," she said, drawing in a deep breath, "I'll do it."

Five

"If I hadn't heard it with my own ears," Chris said breathlessly, "I don't think I ever would have believed it."

"I know exactly what you mean, Chris," Susan returned in the same astonished tone.

The Pratt twins had just sneaked out of City Hall, unseen by anyone, and headed back to the place where their bicycles were stashed. Slowly they were walking them across the lawn, back to the street. While they had begun this phase of their investigation with optimism and energy, at the moment they were both feeling completely deflated.

"I mean, I always knew that Felicia Harris was capable of doing some pretty nasty things," Chris went on, "but never in a million years did I dream that she could stoop so low. Do you know what I keep asking myself, Sooz?"

"No, Chris. What?"

"How anybody could be so darned *selfish*!"

Susan nodded in agreement. "And do you know what I keep asking myself, Chris?"

"What, Sooz?"

"What you and I are going to do about it!"

Chris brightened immediately. "You know, Sooz, I've been so upset about the conversation between Clark and Felicia that we just overheard that I almost forgot that you and I are working on figuring out this whole mess." Then she frowned. "But instead of us getting to the bottom of the mysterious threatening note that was sent to Mayor Harris, we're just getting more and more confused."

"It's true that nothing is making very much sense," Susan admitted. "It doesn't seem to add up, does it? We know that some organization called the Pearson Corporation is buying up all the land it can out on Old Woods Road. And we know that somebody is trying to scare the mayor into changing his mind about the development project. . . ."

"Or else make him look so bad that he'll lose the election next fall. . . ."

"Or both," Susan concluded.

"And we know one more thing," said Chris.

"What's that?"

"That mean old Felicia plans to go ahead with Clark's plan of publicly accusing old Mr. Krigley of having sent that threatening note to the mayor, whether he's actually responsible or not." Chris thought for a few seconds. "Sooz, what we need to do next is find out whether or not the old man is guilty."

Susan's eyes grew wide. "And how do you propose that we do that?"

There was a look of real determination in Chris's brown eyes as she got on her bicycle. "Why, let's go talk to him, of course."

The big ramshackle old house on Old Woods Road that was known locally as the Krigley place had been a curiosity for as long as the Pratt twins could remember. When they were younger, they used to ride by on their bicycles all the time, usually speculating about the spooky house—and the strange old man who lived inside, someone who was rumored never to come out, never to speak to his neighbors, never to have anything to do with anyone. Not only had the twins never talked to him; they had never even dared to venture onto his property.

Now, however, they were about to pay him a visit.

"It's kind of creepy, don't you think?" Chris said with a loud gulp. She and her sister climbed off their bikes and leaned them against the rotting wooden fence that surrounded Mr. Krigley's property. As they did, one of the posts gave way, splitting into two jagged pieces.

"I don't think it's *creepy*, exactly," Susan replied, trying as hard as she could to sound cheerful. "It's just run-down, that's all. Try to picture it with a fresh coat of paint, some flowers planted along the front, some bright blue shutters on all the windows. . . ."

Picturing the house in that way was no easy task. In fact, at the moment, doing so would have required a lot more imagination than either of the twins happened to possess. Instead, the three-story Victorian house, with its sagging front porch, graying weather-worn shingles, and somewhat spooky widow's watch up on top simply looked unloved, uncared for . . . and downright eerie.

"Well, Sooz, here goes," Chris said, standing up as straight as she could and heading for the front walk. "We've come this far, so there's no turning back now."

The front walk consisted of crumbling pieces of slate that were overgrown in between with weeds. In fact, the entire front yard was badly in need of mowing. Wildflowers had sprung up in various parts of the large square of property. All in all, the area looked untamed and forbidding, like a place that no one ever bothered with.

As the twins stepped onto the wooden front porch, the second step creaked loudly, threatening to break beneath their weight.

"Gosh, Sooz, this place is even worse than it looks from the road," Chris whispered. "It reminds me of the scary old house we saw in that movie we rented for the VCR last summer. Remember? It was about a haunted house where all these terrible things kept happening?"

"I don't think it's scary," Susan replied. "It's just . . . old." She was trying to sound matter-of-fact, but even she was finding it impossible to keep the uncertainty out of her voice.

"Well, Sooz, this is it," said Chris. With that, she stepped up to the front door, reached up for the tarnished brass knocker, and knocked three times.

Inside the house, the noise echoed. The girls stood

on the porch for what seemed a very long time. They were surrounded by silence, except for the occasional chirping of a bird or the soft rushing sound of the wind blowing through the autumn leaves that still clung to the stark black branches of the tall trees in Mr. Krigley's yard.

"Maybe there's nobody inside," Chris whispered. "Maybe we should just forget all about this, turn around and go back home and—"

Just then, there was a loud creaking sound as the heavy front door was pulled open. Two blue eyes peeked out. The expression on the small wrinkled face that surrounded those eyes was unmistakably one of mistrust.

The blue eyes immediately grew narrow. "What is it?" the old man croaked. His voice sounded harsh, as if he were angry. "What do you want?"

"Mr. Krigley?" Susan said politely. She swallowed hard. "Are you Mr. Krigley, the owner of this house?"

"Who wants to know?" the man returned sharply.

"Well, uh, my name is Susan Pratt and, uh, this is my sister Christine and, uh—"

"Look here, Mr. Krigley," Chris interrupted impatiently. "We're here to help you out. Somebody in town is on the verge of stirring up a little trouble, and we just wanted to tell you about it before it's too late."

The old man blinked. He hesitated for only a moment, then said in a slightly less crusty voice, "Well, then, I suppose you'll be wanting to come in."

He was muttering to himself as he opened the door

and stepped back. Chris and Susan exchanged looks that were both surprised and pleased. And then, with a nod to the old man, they went inside.

The interior of the house was in the same condition as the exterior. The front parlor, the room in which the girls now found themselves, was dominated by an overstuffed couch trimmed with satin fringe. Tossed onto it were torn brocade pillows. The furniture was wood, the surfaces scuffed and dull. Everything in the room looked worn-out, dusty, and very, very old.

The most outstanding feature of the room, however, was the countless photographs that lined every square inch of wall space, every flat surface, every place that could possibly accommodate a picture frame. Most of them were black-and-white, looking as if they had been taken long ago.

There were photographs of people laughing together, posing in old-fashioned bathing suits and elaborate lace wedding dresses. There were children and old people, newlyweds and newborn babies, groups of friends and clusters that could only be family. What struck the twins most was that they all looked as if they belonged together, as if they were all linked somehow. And above all, the people in the photographs looked extremely happy.

"Now, what's all this about trouble?" Mr. Krigley asked with a frown. "And what do you care, anyway? What's it to you?"

"We're just trying to be helpful, that's all," Susan explained gently. "My sister and I grew up in this town, and we've been fascinated by this place of yours ever since we were children."

"We've always been a little bit curious about you, too," Chris couldn't resist interjecting.

"We're curious about all our neighbors," Susan was quick to add, casting her twin a warning look. "We've always welcomed the chance to get to know as many people here in Whittington as we could."

"All right, all right," the man scowled. "I see what you're saying. You're just a pair of busybodies, that's all. Now what's all this about trouble?"

Susan took a deep breath. "Mr. Krigley, last night the mayor was scheduled to give a speech on television. A speech saying that he was against a plan to knock down the houses here on Old Woods Road and turn this area into a shopping center."

"Yes, I know all about that plan," Mr. Krigley barked. "I read the newspapers, too, you know."

"He never did give his speech," Chris went on. "Just before he was supposed to give it, he received a threatening note. We think it was from someone who was in favor of that plan."

"Mr. Krigley," Susan asked in a soft voice, "how do you feel about that plan? Are you eager to sell this house and move someplace that's . . . someplace newer?"

"What are you talking about?" Mr. Krigley exploded, his eyes opening wide and his face turning red. "Do you think I want to give up this house? I was born in this house. I've lived in it for almost eighty-three years. I was married right here in this parlor, sixty-two years ago. My three children were born in the bedroom upstairs. My grandchildren came to this house for Christmas every year, until they all moved far away.

"Why, this house has been in my family for six generations. My grandparents made this place home back when this town was nothing more than a dozen farms and a general store. This house is my life."

With that, he went over to one of the walls that was filled with photographs and began to mutter.

As Chris and Susan looked at each other, neither was surprised to see that there were tears in the other's eyes.

"Mr. Krigley, we're only trying to help," Susan said in a quiet voice.

"And we *are* going to help," Chris said with a nod.

She happened to glance down then, wanting to keep Mr. Krigley from feeling as if they were watching his every move. As she did, something on a table caught her eye. It was a handwritten note, written in the shaky, uncertain scrawl of a very old person. It had undoubtedly been written by Mr. Krigley . . . and it provided the final piece of evidence she needed to prove to herself that Mr. Krigley couldn't possibly be the person responsible for that threatening note. She could hardly wait to tell Susan.

"Mr. Krigley," she said, for the moment turning her attention back to the old man, "I promise you that my sister and I going to do everything we can to make sure that that land development plan doesn't go through. You can be sure of that."

Mr. Krigley just looked over at her and nodded.

Chris wasn't even sure whether or not he had been listening to her.

But there were two things she *was* perfectly sure of. The first, of course, was that there was no way Mr. Krigley could have possibly been the one to send that threatening note to Mayor Harris. Aside from having met the old man personally and drawn that conclusion based on what she had seen, she now had tangible proof as well. And the second thing was that it was imperative that she and her twin do everything in their power to keep Felicia from going on television and saying that poor Mr. Krigley was guilty.

Fozzy's Ice Cream Parlour, one of the Pratt twins' favorite Whittington hangouts, was empty late that Saturday morning. The Civic Association pancake breakfast was still going on, and from the looks of things, just about everybody in town was still over at the Community Center, eating pancakes and helping the town raise money for the construction of a new playground.

"What's the matter, don't you girls like pancakes?" the twins' waitress, the only other person in the place, teased as she brought two menus over to the table at which Susan and Chris were sitting.

"I like pancakes, but I like coming here even better," Chris returned.

It was true that she was quite fond of this place. Like her twin, she always enjoyed the pink-and-white striped wallpaper and the same charming atmosphere as a real old-fashioned ice-cream parlor.

And not only did Fozzy's serve ice cream; it also served sandwiches, French fries, and the best cheeseburgers in town.

As a matter of fact, it was a cheeseburger that Susan found herself in the mood for as she and her sister sat at their table dejectedly, staring at their menus and trying to act cheerful for each other's benefit even though they were both feeling troubled.

"I guess I'll have one of your famous cheeseburgers," Susan told the waitress. Glancing at her wristwatch, she added, "After all, it *is* almost lunchtime."

Chris studied her menu thoughtfully. Without looking up, she said, "I think I'll have a strawberry milk shake."

"A strawberry milk shake!" Susan exclaimed. "For lunch?"

"Actually, I'm still working on breakfast," Chris returned. "Besides," she added with a shrug, "ice cream always helps me think better."

"In that case," Susan said with a rueful smile, "you'd better have Fozzy's twelve-scoop Ice Cream Avalanche. Right now, you and I have to do some pretty creative thinking . . . and *fast*."

"It's true," Chris agreed with a sigh. "We're in a real pickle. It's obvious that Mr. Krigley is about to be framed . . . by someone who's an absolute expert at that kind of thing, no less. And Sooz, I'm one hundred percent certain that he's innocent."

Susan was startled. "Gee, Chris, I'm pretty sure Mr. Krigley could never had sent that threatening note, too. But you sound even more certain than I am."

Chris's eyes grew round. "Sooz, while I was at his house, I saw something that totally convinces me of his innocence. It was a note he had written to himself. He'd left it on a table, and I just happened to see it."

"A note?" Susan asked excitedly. "What did it say?"

"It said, 'Look into damp basement business.' "

Susan thought for a few seconds, then said, "Chris, just because the poor old man happens to have a damp basement doesn't have anything to do with—"

"Listen, there's more. Sooz, he spelled 'business' wrong. He spelled it 'b-u-s-n-e-s-s.' Don't you get it? Whoever is responsible for that threatening note knew the correct way to spell business . . . and Mr. Krigley obvious doesn't!"

"Gee, you're right," Susan said. Then she grew angry. "Chris, that poor old man really *is* innocent. And he'd be devastated if he were ever arrested, especially for a crime he never committed."

"Yes, he certainly would. And that's why we have to do something to stop it from happening."

"And we have to do it right away, too." Susan glanced at her wristwatch once again. "At three o'clock this afternoon, in less than three and a half hours, Felicia Harris is going to go on TV and tell the world that he's responsible for committing a crime that he simply could not have committed."

"So the Lollipop Plot continues," Chris said without very much enthusiasm. "But to tell you the truth, I haven't got a single idea about where to go from here."

"Let's try to be optimistic," Susan suggested. "So far, we've done a pretty good job."

"It's true." Chris had to admit that, so far, they had put in a full and productive morning, and they had uncovered quite a bit about the mystery surrounding the mayor's anonymous threat. "You have to admit, that was pretty clever of me, telling the janitor over at city hall that I was Felicia. Imagine. He actually believed that I was the mayor's daughter. Of course, he had no reason *not* to believe me, when you think about it. I mean, somebody shows up at the door, claiming to be somebody . . . why *shouldn't* he have believed me? It's not every day that people go around trying to pass themselves off as somebody they're not—" Suddenly, she stopped in midsentence. "Sooz, am I just getting overly sensitive, or it is true that you're not listening to a single word I'm saying?"

Across the table, her twin sister was wearing an odd look. Her dark brown eyes were glazed, and her mouth was twisted into a strange smile.

When she finally spoke, her voice was so soft that Chris could barely hear her.

"Chris, I've got it."

"What, Sooz? I'm not sure I understand what you—"

"I've got it. The perfect plan."

Chris opened her mouth to demand that her twin tell her the idea *immediately*. But just then the waitress reappeared at their table.

"That was fast," Susan commented congenially, smiling at the waitress.

The young woman shrugged as she set down the girls' food in front of them. "The truth is, you two girls are the only people in the place. It's easy to get good service when you're the only customers."

The moment she had left their table, Chris said, "Susan Pratt, don't you dare *touch* that cheeseburger until you've told me your idea. You can't expect me to wait a minute longer."

"All right, then. I won't make you wait at all," Susan said calmly. With deliberate movements she unfolded the paper napkin beside her plate and arranged it in her lap. "The plan is so simple that I'm surprised we didn't think of it sooner. Chris, you're going to pretend that you're Felicia Harris."

Chris just looked at her twin as if she had just begun speaking in another language.

"Sooz, I don't get it. For one thing, I thought I did that already."

"That's right, you did. And you just said yourself that it worked like a charm."

"Well, it did. But I still don't see what—"

"Chris," Susan interrupted in a low, steady voice, "you're going to pretend you're Felicia this afternoon so that you, and *not* the real Felicia, can go on WIT-TV this afternoon at three o'clock in her place."

Chris just stared at her sister for a few seconds. And then her eyes grew wide as the full impact of what her sister was saying hit her.

"I get it," she said breathlessly. "If *I* go on TV, pretending that I'm Felicia, that'll keep her from going on the air and lying about Mr. Krigley being responsible for that threatening note."

"Exactly," Susan nodded "*Now* can I eat my cheeseburger?"

"Wait a minute. Not so fast." Already Chris's expression had darkened. "It seems to me that there are still a couple of details that need to be worked out."

"We can work them out while I'm eating," Susan insisted. With that, she took a big bite of her cheeseburger.

"Okay." Chris leaned over to take a sip of her strawberry milk shake before continuing. "First of all, this business of my pretending that I'm Felicia. If I go on TV pretending to be the mayor's daughter, isn't there a good chance that somebody watching will realize that I'm an imposter and call the station to let them know there's something strange going on?"

Susan thought for a minute. "Normally, I'd say that that was something we would have to worry about. But you're forgetting one thing—something that's pretty much guaranteed to take care of that problem."

"What's that?" Chris blinked.

"This afternoon is the big Homecoming game. Whittington High School is playing Elmsford High School in the most important football game of the season. There's been a huge rivalry between those two schools for as long as I can remember. That means just about everybody in town will be there. Not only people from Whittington, either; people who live in Elmsford will be there, too." Meaningfully she added, "People like Felicia's sorority sisters from Alpha Beta Alpha."

Chris brightened. "You're right! Everyone will be at the game at three o'clock. *Especially* Felicia's friends. In fact, hardly anyone at all will be at home watching TV.''

"Right. And both Clark and the mayor will be tied up at the district attorney's office, probably trying to convince him that Mr. Krigley is responsible, too.'' Susan helped herself to some more of her cheeseburger. "Any other possible problems you can think of?''

Chris was about to drink more milk shake when she suddenly froze. "Yes, as a matter of fact. A *major* one, in fact.''

Susan frowned.

"Sooz, what about Felicia? What are we going to do with her? She's all set to go on TV in a few hours. What about *that*?''

Susan put down her cheeseburger. "Gee, Chris, you're right. I forgot all about the *real* Felicia. And that's probably the most important thing.'' Suddenly she looked crestfallen. "Maybe this plan won't work, after all—''

"Not unless we can stash Felicia away somewhere for a few hours. And I can't imagine that we'd be able to accomplish *that* very easily.''

The two girls were silent for a long time. Then each one of them turned back to her food, eating slowly. They were thoughtful as they ate, trying hard to come up with some solution to this seemingly insurmountable problem. But there just didn't seem to be any way out.

Finally their waitress came back, smiling brightly.

"Can I get you girls anything else?'' she asked. Jokingly she added, "It's not as if I have anything else to do. Boy, I don't think I've ever seen this place so empty before. One thing about this town: everybody really rallies together when there's a fund-raiser or some other kind of civic event.''

She sighed. ''What we needed here was a way of luring people away from that pancake breakfast. We should have told people that we'd be giving away free ice cream to everybody who came in this morning. Hey, I have an even better idea. We should have told people that the location of the pancake breakfast had been switched. That they were supposed to come *here* this morning, instead of the Community Center.''

She was chuckling over her outrageous idea as she placed the girls' check on the table and strolled away, wiping tables that were already perfectly clean just to give herself something to do.

As soon as she was out of earshot, Chris began jumping up and down in her seat.

''Sooz, that's it. There's our solution.''

Susan was puzzled. ''What are you talking about, Chris?''

''That waitress gave me the perfect way to keep Felicia out of our hair long enough for me to go on TV, pretending that I'm the mayor's daughter.''

''I'm afraid I still don't follow—''

''Sooz, while I'm heading over to the TV station, you'll track down Felicia and tell her the location of the interview had been changed.''

''Chris, you're a genius! That *is* a great idea.''

''Well, it wasn't really my idea, but no matter. . . .
I know, how about if you tell Felicia that the television

people decided at the last minute that it would be much more interesting if she were interviewed on location, instead of at the station?''

''I like that, Chris.'' Susan was nodding in agreement. ''It makes perfect sense. I'm certain that Felicia will fall for it. Now, where should we tell her to go?''

Chris was thoughtful as she racked her brain, trying to come up with someplace that made sense, but was far enough away that if she ever did figure out that something was up, she wouldn't have time to get over to the station until after it was too late. And then she snapped her fingers.

''I've got it. Marbury's Department Store. You know, over in the Elmsford Shopping Mall.''

''The store where Katy Johnson is working.'' Susan was beaming. ''That's perfect. I'll tell Felicia that that's where she's supposed to go, and I'll take her over there myself. There'll be enough going on at the mall that I can come up with a distraction if I need it. I can pretend I've just seen a dress that I simply have to have, or decide that I have to get myself one of those big pretzels right away. . . . It's ideal, Chris.''

''All right, then. We'd better get moving.'' Already Chris was counting out money to leave on the table. ''You and I have a lot to do. You have to find Felicia and lure her over to the Elmsford Mall. And I have to get dressed up so I can pretend I'm Felicia.''

Suddenly Chris thought of something else.

''Gee, Sooz,'' she said, making a funny face, ''I'm going to be on television!''

''Don't worry, you'll be great,'' Susan reassured her. ''Besides, if you end up looking silly, it'll really be *Felicia* who'll be embarrassed. After all, that's who everyone will think you are!''

"At least we hope so," Chris said ruefully.

But her nervousness was short-lived. "Come on, Sooz," she suddenly cried. "We've got a busy afternoon ahead of us, so we'd better get going. The Lollipop Plot continues, full speed ahead!"

Six

"*Felicia! There you are. Oh, I'm so glad I found you.*"

Susan was breathless as she dashed across the main meeting room of Whittington's Community Center. It was already after noon, and the pancake breakfast was just about over. By this point only a handful of people remained. The long tables that had been set up just for the occasion were cluttered with empty plates and coffee cups, all of which were being disposed of in an orderly fashion by a few of the volunteers on the clean-up committee.

Felicia, meanwhile, was at the back of the room, counting the money that had been collected by some of the other volunteers and stuffed into empty cigar boxes.

"Ninety-eight, ninety-nine, one hundred," Felicia

was muttering. "There. I've got a hundred dollars in this box."

It was only then that she looked up. When she saw who it was standing opposite her, the expression on her face immediately changed from one of concentration to one of annoyance.

"Oh, it's you. Chris—or is it Susan?" She sighed, as if she found the entire question intolerably boring. "I can *never* tell the two of you apart. And to tell the truth, most of the time I don't even *care* which one of the darling Pratt twins I'm talking to."

"Actually, I'm Susan." Susan refused to become angry. After all, doing so would not only give Felicia the pleasure of achieving exactly what she was trying to achieve; having an argument with her would only get in the way of the smooth proceedings of the Lollipop Plot.

"All right, then, Susan. If you're here in search of pancakes, I'm afraid you're too late. We just sold off the last batch about fifteen minutes ago. And," she added triumphantly, holding up a fat wad of dollar bills, "we made lots and lots of money. This new playground is going to be super. Why, maybe they'll even name it after me. Uh, I mean, after my *father* . . ."

Her cheeks were turning pink. "After all, he *is* the mayor of this town and all. It's just that since Daddy and I of course have the same last name—"

"I understand what you mean," Susan said patiently. "But you must listen to me, Felicia. What I have to tell you is important, and there isn't much time."

Felicia just looked bored. "My goodness, what could *you* possibly have to say to *me*?" Already she had turned her attention back to her pile of dollar bills. She began sorting and counting and muttering under her breath, acting as if the other girl weren't even there.

But Susan remained undaunted. "You're scheduled to be interviewed by WIT-TV this afternoon, aren't you?"

With that, Felicia perked up. "Why, yes, I am, as a matter of fact." She smiled prettily. But before long her expression darkened. "Wait a minute. How did you know that? I don't remember getting the chance to mention it last night when we were talking at the fair. . . ."

"No, you didn't mention it then. But, uh, I was just over at the TV station, and—"

"What on earth were *you* doing there?"

"Oh, I was, uh, trying to see about a summer job for next year." Susan was doing some quick thinking, thankful that at times like this, when the pressure was on, she could usually come up with a way to wangle her way out of even the stickiest spots. "You know, I'm very interested in art, and I was trying to find out whether they could use . . . a set designer."

"I see." Felicia was already losing interest.

"Well, there's been a sudden change in plans as far as your TV appearance is concerned." Susan knew full well that a statement like that was guaranteed to capture Felicia's interest.

"What do you mean?" Felicia was alarmed. "My TV interview hasn't been cancelled, has it?"

"No, no, nothing like that," Susan was quick to reassure her. "The location has changed, that's all. Instead of interviewing you at the station, the TV people have decided that it would be much more interesting for their viewers if the interview was done on location.

"When I mentioned that I knew you," she went on, "they asked me if, as a favor to them, I'd track you down and tell you about the change. They wanted to make sure you didn't waste any of your precious time going to the wrong place."

"Yes, it's true that I *am* a very busy person," Felicia said loftily. "What with my sorority and my volunteer activities and my classes, of course. And then there's my *extremely* active social life. Where are they interviewing me, anyway?"

"At the Elmsford Shopping Mall. In Marbury's Department Store, as a matter of fact."

Felicia considered that bit of news for a few seconds. Finally she said, "Well, that doesn't sound like such a bad idea. Besides, maybe while I'm there I can pick up a new necklace to wear on TV. Daddy still owes me a birthday present. I feel like something gold."

"That sounds lovely, Felicia, but we'd really better get over there soon."

"We? What do you mean, 'we'? "

"Uh, the TV people asked me to escort you over there." In a sudden burst of creativity, she added, "I understand that they provide personal escorts for all their celebrity guests. Just in case they need anything."

Felicia immediately softened. "Now, isn't that sweet of them. They sound like very considerate people."

"We can take my car," Susan offered. "Actually, it's my father's car, but he's agreed to let me use it this weekend." That was one of the very first statements Susan had made since coming into the community center that was actually true.

"Well, all right. But we have to stop off at my house, first. I must change my clothes."

"That's okay, Felicia, but we do have to hurry." Flashing her biggest, most genuine smile, Susan added, "After all, the television people won't be able to wait for us if we're late. As the old saying goes, the show must go on!"

As Felicia followed her out of the community center toward the parking lot, Susan was marveling over how smoothly this first leg of this afternoon's theatrics had gone.

Now, she thought with a rueful smile, if only the rest proceeds without a hitch.

While Susan was in her father's car, driving Felicia to the Elmsford Shopping Mall, Chris was climbing into her mother's car so that she could head over to the WIT-TV station. She had hurried home immediately after leaving Fozzy's. She showered and changed into a simple light blue dress, accessorized it with a colorful scarf tied jauntily at the neck, and fastened a pretty tortoiseshell barrette into her hair. And then she was off.

As she drove off toward the television station, she

discovered that she was actually getting nervous. Whether that was because she was about to try to convince a bunch of people she did not know that she was the daughter of the mayor of Whittington or because she was about to appear on television, she couldn't say.

"It doesn't matter *why* you're nervous," Chris told herself firmly as she pulled the car into the parking lot at the TV station and maneuvered it into a space. "What matters is that you've got to put your nervousness aside. You're trying to accomplish something very important here, remember? Your mission is to protect poor old Mr. Krigley. And feeling nervous isn't going to help you achieve that, not one bit. In fact, all it will do is get in your way."

Her nervousness did soon disappear, but not because of the lecture she had given herself. She simply got so wrapped up in playing the part of Felicia Harris that she forgot all about anything besides putting her heart and soul into her newfound role.

"Hello, there. I'm Felicia Harris," she said as she strode into the television station, acting as if she were totally at ease as she approached the very first person she saw. That person happened to be an attractive young woman, very stylishly dressed, who was carrying a clipboard and looked as if she were in a hurry. "I'm scheduled to be interviewed at three o'clock this afternoon." Without having actually made a decision to do so, Chris found herself adopting the same kind of lofty tone that the real Felicia was so fond of using.

It turned out to have been a wise move, too; she realized that as soon as the woman she had addressed smiled and said, "Oh, yes. Hello, Felicia. I'm pleased to be meeting you in person at last. I'm Abby Preston. Remember? We spoke on the phone a few days ago."

"Yes, of course." Chris was grateful that her tone had helped convince this woman that she really was Felicia. So far, at least, everything was proceeding as planned.

"It's good that you're a little bit early," Abbey went on. "Come on inside and I'll introduce you to Elaine Frank. She's the one who'll be conducting the interview. Now, I hope you're not nervous. . . ."

At three o'clock, Chris found herself sitting in a chair opposite Elaine Frank, one of the anchors for WIT-TV's news broadcasts. She was surrounded by cameras, as well as the brightest, hottest lights she had ever seen. But she barely noticed them; she was too busy marveling that she had actually managed to convince everyone here at the station that she really was Felicia Harris. It appeared as if this stage of the Lollipop Plot were going to proceed without a single mishap.

Suddenly she heard the director say, "Five seconds to air time! Five, four, three, two, . . ."

"Welcome to 'What's New,' " the woman sitting opposite her said as she looked right into the camera with the red light. "This is the television program that tells you, our viewers, about all the local news, the news that affects you most directly. I'm Elaine Frank, and today I have the pleasure of welcoming to our show Felicia Harris, a young woman who, aside from being a native of Whittington and a current student at the state college in Elmsford, is the daughter of Mayor Harris, Whittington's mayor. Welcome, Felicia. How are you today?''

Chris swallowed hard. "I'm fine. And I'd like to thank you for inviting me to be on your show."

"We're glad to have you, Felicia." Elaine Frank's expression suddenly grew serious. "Before we talk about all the exciting festivities that are part of Whittington's Homecoming celebration this weekend, there's something I'd like to ask you about. I know it's on our viewers' minds. What I'm talking about, of course," the interviewer went on, leaning forward in her chair, "is the threatening note that your father, Mayor Harris, received last night. It was passed to him just as he was about to give his speech at the Autumn Harvest Festival, the kickoff for the big Homecoming Weekend. It was a warning not to give that speech. Now the police have a full-scale search out as they're trying to find out just who is responsible. Could you please comment on the situation, Felicia?"

"Well, naturally I'm very upset about it."

"Yes, I'm sure you are. But tell us, Felicia, do you have any idea who might be responsible for sending a threatening note to the mayor of your hometown, the man who also happens to be your father?"

Chris drew in a deep breath before speaking. This was the moment she had been geared up for, and she wanted to make sure she answered this question very, very carefully.

"The truth of the matter," she said slowly, "is that I don't know any more about who's responsible than anyone else does."

*   *   *

"Honestly, Felicia, you look just *fine*," Susan reassured her charge for the fourteenth time since the two girls had entered the Elmsford Shopping Mall almost half an hour earlier.

"I know I do," Felicia replied, keeping her eyes fixed on the mirror she had just stopped in front of, this one in the window of a store selling furniture and other things for the home. "I'm just checking, that's all."

With that, the mayor's daughter took one more long look at her reflection. She did, indeed, look nice today, if a bit dramatic. She was dressed in a purple wool dress with oversized sleeves, one that made her look quite sophisticated. Her long blond hair was pulled back into a bun and accessorized with three rhinestone barrettes.

"There," she finally said. "I just wanted to make certain that I look my best for my television appearance, that's all. Don't forget, it's not every day that I'm interviewed on TV. Besides, I've always felt that one's appearance is extremely important. Don't you agree?"

She turned her attention back to Susan then, glancing at her brown wool pants and plain beige sweater with open disapproval. "What time is it, anyway? Shouldn't we be heading over to Marbury's soon?"

"Gosh, you're right." Susan glanced at her watch and pretended to be surprised. "Wow, look at that. It's already ten minutes to three."

"Ten to three!" Felicia cried. "Already? Oh, dear,

we'd better hurry. I just hope my hair doesn't get all mussed up.''

Susan, of course, had absolutely no desire to hurry. She knew full well that when she and Felicia got to the Junior Sportswear section at Marbury's Department Store there would be no cameras, no lights, and no TV people. And she, in turn, would be faced with the problem of how to explain it all to Felicia.

Fortunately for Susan, this was turning out to be another one of those occasions when being forced to think under pressure served her well. By the time she and Felicia reached the displays of sweaters, blouses, and corduroy pants, she had figured out the perfect way to handle this situation. She was going to act just as baffled as Felicia.

"Gosh, Felicia, where *is* everybody?" she asked, blinking as she pretended to be surprised.

"What are you asking *me* for?" Felicia returned. "*You're* the one who's supposed to be the expert here! Oh, darn, is that a snag in my pantyhose? Yes, it is! *Now* look what you've done!"

"Felicia, I haven't done a thing to make your pantyhose snag," Susan replied calmly. "Besides, there's no reason to get all upset. I'll just find a pay phone and call the station. I'm sure there's some perfectly reasonable explanation for all this."

"And what am *I* supposed to do in the meantime?" Felicia demanded.

"I know. Why don't you go buy yourself a brand-new pair of pantyhose? And you can check out Marbury's jewelry counter while you're at it. Didn't you mention something about wanting a new necklace to wear on television?''

With that, Susan was off. She walked toward the escalator, going through the motions of heading up to the second floor where she knew the pay phones were located, right near the restrooms. On her way, she passed through the Children's Department, and she ran right smack into Katy Johnson.

''Katy! What on earth are *you* doing here?'' She had become so wrapped up in keeping Felicia distracted and out of Chris's way that she was startled by the sight of someone she knew.

''I work here, remember?'' Katy laughed. ''And where are you headed, looking so determined?''

''Oh, Katy, it's a long story,'' Susan replied with a sigh. ''I wish I had time to tell you all about it, but right now I'm in the middle of something very important.''

''Really?'' Katy's face lit up. ''You're not busy with one of your little sleuthing adventures, are you?''

''Well . . . I really can't go into it right now, Katy.''

Her friend nodded knowingly. ''I get it, Susan. I understand completely. But let me just say one thing. If there's anything I can do for you, anything at all, just let me know, okay?''

Five minutes later, Susan was back in the Junior Sportswear Department, wearing the biggest smile she could manage. Felicia looked up at her expectantly. It appeared that she had used the last ten minutes efficiently. Not only was she wearing a brand-new pair of pantyhose, one without a single snag; there was also a new gold necklace around her neck.

"My, isn't that beautiful," Susan commented.

Felicia just waved her hands in the air. "Forget all that, Susan. What did you find out? Where are those TV people, anyway?"

"Oh, there's just been a tiny mix-up, that's all. They forgot to tell me back at the station that when they changed the location of your TV interview, they also changed the time. It's going to be at five o'clock instead of three o'clock. There's another small change, too," she added, glancing around and noting that the saleswoman who worked in Junior Sportswear was looking at them strangely, no doubt wondering why these two girls who obviously weren't shopping for anything in particular were spending so much time hanging around in her department. "The interview is going to take place in the Junior Dress Department."

"Not until five o'clock." Felicia groaned. "You mean we have to hang around here for another two hours?"

"It's not as if it won't be worth it," Susan reminded her. "You *are* going to be on TV, after all. Besides, that'll give us plenty of time to do some more shopping. . . . Felicia, look at that outfit over there. My goodness, it looks as if it were made with you in mind, doesn't it? That color is just perfect for you."

For the next two hours, Susan dragged Felicia around the mall, constantly picking out things that she hoped would capture the other girl's interest. They spent a full fifteen minutes trying on virtually every hat in Marbury's Hat Department, sampled twenty-three different shades of pink lipstick as Felicia searched for just the right one, and pored over every single fashion magazine on display at the mall's bookstore. They look at the puppies at Pet World, tried on boots at The Cobbler's Shoppe, and had not one but two ice cream cones.

All in all, spending the afternoon with Felicia reminded Susan of baby-sitting. She was willing to do almost anything she could think of to please Felicia, just to keep her happy . . . and busy. She only hoped that in keeping her out of the way, she was giving her twin enough time to go on TV, successfully pull off her charade of pretending that *she* was Felicia Harris, and to allow "the mayor's daughter" to appear on television without using the opportunity to publicly accuse an innocent man of a terrible crime.

Finally, it was fifteen minutes before five.

"Let's go back to Marbury's *now*," Felicia insisted. "I want to get there early this time. I intend to make sure that this TV appearance of mine doesn't run into any more complications."

Susan watched Felicia's face fall a little while later as she went sailing into the Junior Dress Department with Susan in tow—and once again there were no cameras, no lights, not even a single wire.

"Susan Pratt, what is going on here?" she demanded, stamping her foot. There were tears in the girl's eyes as she struggled to make some sense out of the confusing events of the day—and to deal with the emotional ups and downs she had experienced as a result.

Susan would have been getting nervous about what to do next if she weren't feeling so sorry for Felicia. It was obvious that being on TV was very important to her, yet Susan and her sister had cheated her out of her big opportunity. It was only after she had reminded herself of what Felicia had been intending to *do* while she had the public's attention that she was able to put things back in perspective.

"Look, Felicia, you wait here. I'll go call the station again. Surely there's a good explanation for this. . . ."

She hurried off, once again heading toward the escalator. This time, however, she really did go over to the pay phones. She dropped in some change and dialed the number of her own home.

"Hello, Chris? It's me," she said breathlessly. "I'm still at the mall. Felicia doesn't seem to suspect anything, but she's getting itchy. How did it go—and what should I do now?"

"Oh, Sooz," Chris returned. "The TV interview went perfectly. The people at the station really believed that I was the mayor's daughter. That part went fine. But I still need more time."

"More time!" Susan cried. "Chris, what am I supposed to—"

"Sooz, if Felicia finds out *now* what happened, she'll be furious. And I have no doubt that she'll go straight to the TV station . . . or maybe even to the police. For all we know, she might demand that Mr. Krigley be arrested immediately. Look, I have to find out who's responsible for sending that note—and fast. We may have bought ourselves more time by this afternoon's bit of trickery, but there's still more work to be done before we're through!''

Susan sighed. "All right, Chris. I hear what you're saying. You need me to keep Felicia out of your hair as long as I can."

"Oh, I knew you'd come through, Sooz! You're a gem!"

When Susan hung up the telephone a few seconds later, she was totally dejected. She had just spent an entire afternoon keeping Felicia distracted, and now, just when she thought she was about finished with the ordeal of spending all that time in the company of someone she could barely stand, she had to come up with an entirely new way of keeping Felicia safely tucked out of the way. She was exhausted . . . and she was completely out of ideas.

It was while she was ruminating about her predicament that someone tapped her on the shoulder. She jumped about three feet in the air.

"Oh, Katy. It's you."

"That's right, it's me," Katy returned with a grin. "I've got a ten-minute break, and I was heading over to the water fountain. The store hasn't been too busy today, but even so, I'm pretty tired. Good thing we're closing in an hour."

Suddenly Susan's eyes opened wide. "Katy, what did you just say?"

The other girl looked puzzled. "Oh, nothing important, Susan. I just said that the store closes in an hour."

Slowly a big smile crept across Susan's face.

"Katy," she said, "do you remember the offer you

made before? You said that if there was anything you could do to help me out, I just needed to ask, right?''

She put her arm around her friend's shoulder. ''Well, it turns out that there is something you can do.''

Seven

The bright November sun was low in the sky as Chris headed toward city hall for the second time that day, once again in search of information. This time, rather than arriving on a bicycle, she was traveling by car. She took care to park a few blocks away to keep from arousing any suspicion.

As she hurried across the front lawn, nervously glancing over her shoulder every few seconds to make sure no one saw her, she was suddenly struck with a disheartening realization.

"Oh, no," she muttered. "All the doors are bound to be locked, just like they were earlier today. How on earth am I going to get in?"

She glanced at her watch, then quickened her pace. It was ten minutes before five. Maybe, just maybe, if her streak of good luck held out, that same janitor would still be around.

After trying four different doors to city hall, shouting as loudly as she could, and banging on each one without getting any response, she tried one of the side doors. Sure enough, right inside, one of the hall lights was on. The same good-natured janitor who had let her in only a few hours before was still there, this time polishing doorknobs.

I fooled that poor man once, Chris was thinking as she knocked loudly and began yelling, "Hello! Hello!" Now, if only I can manage to pull it off one more time.

She saw immediately that she wasn't about to have the slightest problem accomplishing just that.

"Why, hello, again," the janitor called, smiling broadly and waving with his polishing cloth.

"Please let me in," Chris said. "There's something I forgot to get before."

The janitor wasted no time in coming over to the door to unlock it.

"It's nice to see you again, Ms. Harris," he said as he stepped aside to let Chris into the building. Shyly, he added, "You know, I saw you on television before."

"You did!" Chris was startled. She held her breath, waiting to see what he would say next.

"Yes, it sure was exciting to see somebody I actually know on TV. See, I was taking my three o'clock break, and there's a television set downstairs, an old black-and-white one some of us on the cleaning crew have set up in the boiler room. I went down there, made myself a cup of coffee, put my feet up, and switched on the set. And there you were!

"Of course," he added, "I'm afraid there weren't a lot of other people watching. I have a feeling that just about everybody around these parts was over at the big Homecoming game today."

"That's all right," Chris said quickly. "It was still fun to have the chance to be on television." Trying to sound casual, she asked, "So what did you think, anyway?"

The man brightened. "Why, you did a fine job. A real fine job. You seemed so comfortable being on TV. I guess it's because you're already so used to being in the public eye."

"I guess that must be it," Chris agreed with a somber nod.

"By the way, I'm real sorry about your dad. That threatening note he got and all that."

"Thank you."

"And you know, I didn't notice this the first time I saw you, but you really are the spitting image of your father. You and your father the mayor are dead ringers."

Chris just smiled. "I know. People are always telling me that. Now, if you'll excuse me, I really have to run upstairs and pick up something I forgot."

With that, she headed toward the stairs, keeping her hand near her face to hide the fact that she couldn't quite keep herself from chuckling.

While Chris was acting as if she knew exactly where she was going, the truth was that she didn't really know what she was looking for . . . or where to begin looking for it. She simply had a feeling that there could well be something in this building that would provide her with a clue as to who had sent the threatening note to Mayor Harris. Besides, the truth of the matter was that aside from City Hall, she didn't have a single idea about where else to look.

She was heading toward Mayor Harris's office when one of the other offices on the way suddenly caught her eye.

"Clarkson P. Rutherford III, Assistant to Mayor Harris," were the hand-lettered words on the frosted glass panel inset into the wooden door.

Chris stopped dead in her tracks. Clark. Of course. He *had* to have something to do with all this. After all, he was the one who was so anxious to have Felicia go on TV and lie about what she had seen at the fair the night before. He had concocted the whole story. He must have had a good reason to be so involved.

Perhaps Clark knew something. Maybe he was covering something up. At any rate, Chris certainly intended to try to find out.

Slowly, stealthily, holding her breath as if she were afraid of what she might discover, Chris tried the doorknob of Clark's office. When it moved easily in her hand, telling her that the door hadn't been locked, she didn't know whether to be glad or sorry.

You've come this far, she reminded herself. You're not about to back off now. Not when you might be on the trail of something important—something that will magically make all the pieces fit together.

She closed the door behind her. It was difficult to see in the twilight, and she hesitated before switching on a light. Then she remembered how fully convinced the janitor was that she was the mayor's daughter.

After all, he had even seen her on television! Smiling, she decided that there was no reason to worry.

Chris felt a little guilty as she opened the drawers of Clark's filing cabinet, one at a time, and peeked inside. Not that she actually looked through them, or did anything more than give the contents a quick glance. It was just that she felt bad thinking ill of him. After all, she hardly knew him. It was true that he had been working very hard to convince his girlfriend that the threatening note had been sent by a man whom Chris was ninety-nine percent certain was innocent, but maybe he had a good reason.

She was about to slink out of Clark's office, giving in to her guilt and concluding that she was being too quick to make judgments about somebody else's character, when in truth she had very little to go on, when she happened to open the top drawer of his desk. She started. While she had expected to see only paper clips and pencils in there, instead what was staring her right in the face, balanced on top of all the office supplies arranged neatly inside, was a plain white envelope. Written on it in small precise letters was the name Clarkson Rutherford.

Chris froze. So far, she hadn't done anything besides poke around Clark's office a bit. She hadn't really been snooping. Opening this envelope, however, would definitely put her into the "snoop" category. She held it in her hand, just staring at it, wondering what to do.

And then the image of Mr. Krigley staring at the wall full of photographs came into her mind. She could picture the tears in the old man's eyes, and she could hear him saying, "This house is my life."

No, it was impossible that he was guilty, even aside from Susan's discovery about his inability to spell the word "business" correctly. But Clarkson Rutherford wanted everyone to believe that he was.

She opened up the envelope, suddenly very eager to see what was inside.

Once she did, she gasped. While she may not have actually been holding an incriminating piece of evidence in her hands, she knew that at long last she was onto something.

In the envelope was a check for five thousand dollars, made out to cash. It was signed by someone named Alfred J. Pierce. Attached to it with a paper clip was a note, written in what looked like the same handwriting as the signature on the check. It read, "For the special 'work' you performed for me. Good job! A.J.P."

"Alfred J. Pierce," Chris muttered, reading the name off the check.

That name didn't mean very much to her. But she had a funny feeling that it could well have a lot to do with the mystery behind the threatening note and Clark's desire to blame it all on one of the elderly residents of Old Woods Road.

While she didn't recognize the name printed on the check, she did recognize the address. Laughing Brook Road was the address of some of the largest houses in Whittington, houses that were owned by some of the wealthiest, most powerful people in the area.

As for the resident of number Thirteen Laughing Brook Road, Chris had every intention of finding out who he was—and what he had to do with Clark, Mr. Krigley, and Mayor Harris. She also intended to find out what special 'work' this Mr. Pierce had paid Felicia's new boyfriend Clark the royal sum of five thousand dollars to carry out.

Chris was glad she was still dressed up in the outfit she had worn during her television appearance, while masquerading as the mayor's daughter. In her simple blue dress, she looked dignified, grown-up, and extremely trustworthy. And that was exactly the image she wanted to convey as she took a deep breath, held her chin up high, thrust back her shoulders, and confidently strode up the front walk of number Thirteen Laughing Brook Road, a stately red brick mansion with a paved circular driveway, neatly trimmed hedges all around, and, judging from the large number of windows on all three floors, at least eight bedrooms.

She had done some quick thinking as she drove the three miles or so from city hall over to this section of Whittington. She was taking a real chance, acting on not much more than a hunch. But she knew she had to do something, and checking out Alfred J. Pierce seemed like a very good place to start. Besides, by this point, she had her story entirely worked out. She was suitably dressed for the part she intended to play, and she was in a determined frame of mind.

The only thing that remained uncertain at this point

was whether or not she would actually be able to carry off the whole thing.

"Good afternoon," she said to the man who answered the door, peering out at her as if the last thing he was expecting today was a visitor. "Are you Mr. Pierce? Mr. Alfred J. Pierce?"

"Yes, I am," the man replied, sounding a bit gruff. "And if you're selling something, young lady, I can assure you that—"

"Oh, no. I'm not selling anything," Chris was quick to assure him. "My name is Christine Pratt and I'm a member of the Citizens for Local Development League. Surely you've heard of, uh, the C.L.D.L.?"

"As a matter of fact, I haven't," the man said impatiently. "What are you doing, trying to raise money for some pointless civic organization?"

"Actually," Chris said, swallowing hard and hoping that the nervousness she was feeling didn't show, "in addition to being a member of the league, I also happen to be chairperson of a special committee. It's called the Citizens for the Development of Old Woods Road Committee."

Just as she had been hoping, the man reacted strongly to that statement. He actually began smiling. "I see. What can I do for you?"

"To tell you the truth, I have a feeling that there's something that *I* can do for *you*."

"Oh, really?" Alfred Pierce looked skeptical. "And what, may I ask, is that?"

Just talking to this man, studying his reactions, made Chris more certain than ever that the "hunch"

she had been following was correct. She decided to
throw all caution to the wind and jump right in. She
held her head up higher than ever and looked Mr.
Pierce right in the eye.

''Why, what I'm trying to do is help drum up public
support for the development of Old Woods Road. And
I know how important that is to you.''

Sure enough, the look of surprise on the man's face
quickly softened into a smile.

''Well, for heaven's sake, young lady. Come right
in.''

The inside of the house was just as grand as the
outside. The front room, a room that appeared to be a
combination living room and office, was decorated
with expensive-looking antiques, a plush Oriental car-
pet, and thick brocade draperies. There was a big
wooden desk in one corner. At the moment it was
covered with papers and file folders.

Most interesting to Chris, however, were the framed
pictures that were hung all around the room. Instead of
antique photographs or oil paintings, there were photographs of shopping centers, office buildings, and
condominium complexes.

Chris just stared at them as she felt the wheels inside
her head turning. Suddenly it all made sense. This
man, Mr. Alfred J. Pierce, was a land developer. That
explained his interest in the development of Old
Woods Road.

And then another wheel turned. Pierce . . . the Pearson Corporation . . . of course! He was the man who
was buying up the land out there, keeping it a secret so
that land prices would stay down fairly low. He was

the person who wanted to turn that residential area into a shopping center . . . even though the mayor of Whittington was dead set against it.

"Now, young lady, what is it you were saying?" Mr. Pierce sat down at his desk, motioning to his visitor to take a seat on the couch opposite him.

Chris took a deep breath. She needed to get her bearings after what she had already pieced together, even before she had had a chance to talk to this man.

She cleared her throat before speaking. "Mr. Pierce, the organization I represent, the Citizens for the Development of Old Woods Road Committee, is very interested in the economic growth of Whittington. We feel that creating new businesses—building new stores, putting up office buildings, encouraging new businesses to move to our area—can only help us achieve our end. *Progress*, Mr. Pierce. Progress through development. In fact, that's our committee's slogan."

"Go on." Mr. Pierce leaned forward and folded his hands on the desk in front of him.

"I'll get right to the point, Mr. Pierce. I—uh, I mean, *we* are fully aware of your interest in achieving this goal, especially with respect to Old Woods Road."

Mr. Pierce smiled oddly. "Well, of course I am. After all, I *am* the main force behind that project." He stopped, glancing at her with what Chris interpreted to be alarm. "But you already knew that . . . didn't you?"

"I certainly did. And I applaud your efforts. In fact, all of us on the committee are backing you up one hundred percent. We're also in favor of tearing down those . . . those *eyesores* over on Old Woods Road that try to pass themselves off as houses. We all agree that a shopping center in that area would be a real improvement.''

"Wait a minute." Suddenly Mr. Pierce frowned. "How did you know about all this, anyway? My involvement, I mean." His expression darkened. "It was that Rutherford boy, wasn't it? Clark? Is he the one?"

"Let me assure you," Chris said quickly, "that in telling us about your involvement in the Old Woods Road development project, Clark was doing both you *and* us a real favor. You see, uh, we all banded together, uh, those of us who felt Whittington wasn't growing fast enough and, uh, we approached the mayor. We felt he wasn't being responsive to our complaints, but, uh, then Clarkson Rutherford heard about our group. . . .''

Chris's mind was clicking away, constructing a story that she only hoped Mr. Pierce would find believable.

"I see. I'm sure you understand, then, why I've wanted to maintain such secrecy all along. Why it was important that I keep my identity under wraps, buying up land on Old Woods Road under a name that wouldn't readily be associated with me, even employing people on the inside, at city hall, to help make sure the plan would go through. . . .''

Deep inside Chris's head, more pieces of the puzzle suddenly fit together. There it was, as plain as the nose on Mr. Pierce's face.

Clark was working for Mr. Pierce! It was Felicia's boyfriend who was responsible for sending that threatening note to the mayor! He was the person working on the inside, trying to make the Old Woods Road development project go through by making Mayor Harris look bad. He could even have been spying on the mayor, for all she knew, feeding secret information to Alfred Pierce.

Even though it was all enough to make Chris's stomach turn, she had to admit that it made a lot of sense.

And what happened next made the whole picture even clearer.

"And when I run for mayor next year . . ." Mr. Pierce said breezily.

He froze. A look of horror crossed his face, and his voice dropped down to a whisper. "No one is supposed to know about that. At least, not yet."

"Oh, don't worry, Mr. Pierce," Chris said with a casual wave of her hands. Even she herself was startled by the coolness with which she was handling this major discovery that she had just made, thanks to Mr. Pierce's pompousness. "You have quite a following here in town, you know, people who have been watching you for a long time, hoping that one day soon you would be making exactly that announcement. And that brings us back to why I've come here in the first place. Mr. Pierce, I just wanted to tell you you have the full support of the Citizens for Local Development League. We're willing to do anything to help our cause—petitioning, picketing, whatever it takes. And now that I know you'll be running against Mayor Harris in the election next year—a fact that will remain our little secret, I can assure you—I think it would be reasonable for me to speak on behalf of my fellow committee members and offer our help with your campaign.''

"Thank you. Thank you very much.'' Mr. Pierce was beaming.

"And now I'm afraid I have to be going.'' Chris stood up. Her meeting had gone smoothly, and she was satisfied that she had gotten exactly what she had come for.

Almost, anyway.

"Mr. Pierce,'' said Chris, coughing a bit and then clearing her throat, ''may I trouble you for a glass of cold water before I go? My throat is so dry.''

"Of course. No trouble at all. I'll just go into the kitchen and get it.''

Chris called after him, "Could I have an ice cube, please? Make that two. And I'd appreciate it if you'd let the faucet run for a minute to make sure the water is really cold.''

"No problem,'' he called back from the kitchen.

Chris knew she had only a few seconds to act. She hurried over to Alfred Pierce's desk. Knowing what she now knew, she wasn't at all surprised to see that the papers on his desk had to do with his plans for starting up a political campaign to run for mayor of Whittington the following year. In fact, after glancing at three or four, she found one, written in longhand in that same handwriting she had seen before, that outlined his strategy. The first item written on it, underlined three times, was, "Knock Harris out of the race!"

She had just finished tucking it into her purse when Mr. Pierce came back into the room, carrying a glass of ice water.

"Oh, thank you so much," she said, drinking it down in four huge gulps. "Goodness, I didn't realize I was so thirsty. Well, thank you again for your time. Our citizens' group will be in touch soon."

With that, she headed out the door. She couldn't help giving her pocketbook a satisfied tap as she strode out to the car. She had the goods on Mr. Pierce now . . . and it didn't take much imagination to figure out Clarkson Rutherford's role in all this, either. All she had to do now was make sure the people of Whittington found out what she knew—the sooner, the better.

Eight

"Susan Pratt, if you ever tell a single soul about this, I'll . . . I'll . . . Well, frankly, I don't know *what* I'll do. But I can assure you that it'll be something *terrible!"*

Felicia flounced across the dimly lit Shoe Department of Marbury's which, at the moment, had not a single soul inside it aside from Felicia and Susan. The counters had no salespeople behind them, and the cash registers were all locked up. Not one shopper lingered in the aisles. It was six-thirty in the evening, and the two girls were locked inside the department store.

"Don't be too upset, Felicia," Susan said soothingly. "After all, we have plenty of food to eat. We have all the imported cookies and crackers we could possibly want, right here in Marbury's Gourmet Foods Department. We have a dozen beds to choose from in the Furniture Department. And if we get bored, we can always go up to the Book Department. Then there are the televisions upstairs in Small Appliances. And let's not forget the Toy Department.

"Besides," she added with a big smile, "being locked up overnight in Marbury's will give us the chance to get to know each other better."

Despite her pretense of simply trying to make the best of what appeared to be a bad situation, Susan couldn't have been more gleeful. This phase of her plan had gone even more smoothly than she ever could have dreamed.

She had decided that the ideal way of keeping Felicia tucked away and out of trouble long enough for Chris to carry out her sleuthing efforts was to arrange for both herself and the mayor's daughter to get locked into Marbury's after it closed. And making it all happen turned out to be a simple matter.

First she had checked with Katy.

"Well, let's see," Katy said in response to Susan's question about the store's procedure for closing. "It's all pretty straightforward. At six o'clock the doors are locked. No more shoppers can get in after that. Then the employees are supposed to make a quick check around our departments to make sure no one is still inside. And then we sign out and exit through the back door. As far as I know, by six-twenty the store is completely deserted."

"I see," Susan said, nodding as she listened closely to every detail. "What about security guards? Are there any of those walking around the store?"

Katy laughed. "Those guys are gone. Everything is done electronically now, at least here at Marbury's.

There are alarms on every cash register and every door and window, so just as long as no one is trying to take any money or get in or out of the store, there's no way of knowing *what's* going on inside.''

"How about a cleaning crew? Aren't there people in here all night, cleaning the place?''

Katy shook her head. "Not on Saturday nights. The cleaning crew doesn't come in then. They show up early on Sunday mornings and do their work then.''

Katy's eyes grew narrow and she lowered her voice. "Susan, I want you to notice that while I'm telling you everything I know, I'm making a point of not asking you *why* you want to know. I'm assuming that you have your reasons . . . and that they're no business of mine.''

Susan just smiled.

What it all boiled down to was that by six-twenty the store was indeed deserted, just as Katy had promised. Felicia and Susan had the place to themselves, with no easy way out. And that, as far as Susan was concerned, was exactly how she wanted it.

Felicia, of course, didn't know any of this. And Susan was counting on that fact to make sure that she and her charge remained tucked away inside the store for a long, long time.

She was still amazed by how simple it had been to arrange. After her last excursion to the telephones, the one during which she really did call Chris and consult with Katy on the workings of the store, Susan had hurried back down to the main floor. Felicia was still waiting impatiently in the Junior Department.

"What did they say *now*?" she demanded.

Once again, Susan found that she had to feel sorry for the girl. She knew that poor Felicia was bound to be disappointed, and the expression on her face made it clear that she was.

"I'm so sorry, Felicia. They said they had trouble getting their cameras over here. Something about one of them breaking down, and the replacement not fitting in the truck. . . . At any rate, they said they'll simply have to postpone it a little longer, that's all."

"Oh, *no*!"

"I feel really bad, Felicia. The people at the station were very apologetic, but they said it just couldn't be helped."

Suddenly Felicia took off across the Junior Dress Department.

"Show me where the phones are in this stupid store," she demanded. "I'm going to call the station and talk to those people myself."

"Gee, Felicia, I'm afraid you can't do that."

While Susan may have sounded perfectly calm and in control, the truth was that she was on the verge of panic. She had exactly three seconds to come up with a good reason why Felicia couldn't call the WIT-TV station herself.

"Why can't I?" Felicia returned, stopping in her tracks and whirling around.

"Because, uh, they, uh, the woman I've been talking to all along was just about to leave for the day. She was on her way out when I called, in fact. I was lucky I got her at all."

"There must be somebody else I could talk to."

Susan shook her head. "I'm afraid not. She told me that the whole station was practically closing down. You see, apparently they only keep a skeleton crew there on Saturday nights. A handful of technical people who can put on reruns and shows that have already been taped."

She held her breath, searching Felicia's face. She saw the anger and determination fade into disappointment, and she was able to start breathing again. Her excuse had worked. Now if she could only continue . . .

Susan glanced at her watch and saw that it was ten minutes to six. That meant she had to work fast to arrange for herself and Felicia to get locked into Marbury's for this crucial next phase of the Lollipop Plot. And the phase that, at least from where she was standing right now, was definitely the most difficult part.

She looked around, searching for inspiration. And she found it—in the form of a royal blue velvet dress, hanging on a separate rack apart from the dozens of other dresses on display in Marbury's Junior Dress Department.

"Oh, Felicia!" she cooed, rushing over to admire the dress. "*Look* at this dress. Gosh, it's *you*. It's really you."

As an extra added touch, she made a point of adding one more comment. "But look at the price tag. Wow, that's expensive. It's certainly out of my price range."

"Let me see that." Felicia strutted over to look at

the dress that Susan was making such a fuss about. "Hmmm. It *is* kind of nice, isn't it?"

"Felicia, it's perfect for you. Why, that deep color would look wonderful with your blond hair. And the way it's cut would show off your slim figure beautifully."

"Yes, it would, wouldn't it?" Felicia fingered the soft blue fabric.

Susan could tell she was getting hooked. "But look at the price," she said. "It must be the most expensive dress in the whole store."

"Oh, *that* doesn't matter," Felicia said loftily. "Daddy buys me anything I want. It's not important what it costs. He's always saying, 'Felicia, honey, *nothing* is too good for my daughter.' Now let's see. Do they have it in my size?"

Just as Susan had been anticipating, Felicia was too enamored with the dress—or, to be more accurate, her image of how she would look in it—to notice that, all around her, people in the store were getting ready for closing time. Practically all the customers were gone; the few who remained were glancing at their watches as they hurried toward the cash registers to pay for their last-minute purchases. The salespeople were straightening up racks and counters, putting things away, and locking up the cash registers that weren't being used.

Felicia, meanwhile, was heading toward the dressing room, her eyes bright.

"This dress will be perfect for Alpha Beta Alpha's Christmas dance next month. Oh, I hope it's not too long. Of course, I could always hire a dressmaker to shorten it if that's a problem.''

Felicia sailed into the dressing room with Susan a few feet behind her. She didn't even notice that there was no one else in there, not even someone at the door to check them in and out.

''I'll just wait in the dressing room next door,'' Susan said casually. ''I can't wait to see how you look in that dress.''

As Felicia was slipping on the dress, Susan could hear the sounds of the store closing down. At one point, one of the employees stuck her head inside the main entryway to the dressing room, took a quick look around, and called over her shoulder, ''No, there's no one left in here.'' Susan's heart pounded the whole time. But as difficult as it was for her to believe, it actually looked as if she was going to carry this off.

When Felicia came out from behind the curtain of her dressing room a few seconds later, the dress was still unzipped in the back. But from what Susan could tell, it did indeed look fabulous on her.

''Susan, sweetie, I can't quite reach the back. Do you think you could get the zipper on this?'' Felicia asked, never taking her eyes off her reflection.

''Sure. Let me come into the dressing room with you.'' Susan ducked inside, just in case anyone else came by. ''Now let me see that zipper . . . oh, it's stuck.''

''Stuck!''

''Wait a minute; there's a little thread that got in the way. Hold on, I'm getting it, I'm getting it. . . .''

Susan had to admit that she was becoming an expert

at stalling. As she pretended to struggle with the zipper, a zipper that in reality was perfectly fine, it was all she could do to keep from chuckling. She couldn't wait to tell Chris about all this.

"Here we go. I've got it. Oh, Felicia, the dress looks great on you. Here, turn around."

Getting Felicia to spend almost a full ten minutes admiring herself, in every possible pose and from every imaginable angle, was no problem. By that point, Susan knew full well, the store just had to be empty, no doubt on the verge of being locked up for the entire night.

And then, all of a sudden, the lights grew dim.

"Hey, what's going on?" Felicia glanced around, more annoyed than concerned. "How are we supposed to see?"

"It's probably just a brownout," said Susan. "Maybe the people in the area have been using too much electricity, and the lights are going to be dim for a few minutes. Haven't you ever experienced that before?"

But Felicia had already turned her attention back to her reflection. "One thing's for sure. I'm definitely getting this dress."

It was six-twenty by the time Susan and Felicia emerged from the dressing room. They were chatting about the dress when they reached the doorway. And then Felicia froze.

"Wait a minute. Where *is* everybody?"

It was an eerie sight: the first floor of Marbury's dimly lit, empty of activity, totally deserted. It was like a dream, or perhaps a nightmare. At any rate, it was not at all what the mayor's daughter had been expecting.

"What's going on here?" she demanded. "What is this, some kind of joke? Or maybe the TV people . . ."

For a moment, she sounded hopeful as the thought occurred to her that perhaps this peculiar sight had something to do with the fact that a television interview was supposed to take place here. But then she realized that the store was closed.

"Are we locked in here?" Felicia sounded alarmed.

"Don't worry," Susan was quick to reassure her. "If we are, we can get out somehow. Don't be afraid."

"Afraid? I'm not afraid!" Felicia laughed haughtily, as if to show how ridiculous the very idea was. "I was just thinking how silly I'm going to look if word of this ever leaks out. My sorority sisters would never let me hear the end of it if they found out I was stupid enough to get myself locked into a department store."

Felicia's line of reasoning gave Susan new confidence. "We could always call the police. Or we could open one of the fire doors—"

"No way! The last thing I want is for everyone in town to hear about this." She turned to Susan, her eyes glowing with anger. "Susan Pratt, how could you let this happen?"

Susan's eyes opened wide. She was about to counter with a few accusations of her own, but then she remembered that for the next twelve to fifteen hours, she would be locked inside a store with Felicia. So instead she said, "Gosh, Felicia, I guess I just got so caught up in how great you looked in that dress that I didn't notice anything else.''

The girl seemed satisfied with that explanation.

''Well, all right. But what are we going to do now? How can we get out of this place without the whole world knowing about our silly mistake?''

Susan pretended to think for a few seconds. ''I know. I bet that sooner or later a cleaning crew will be coming through here. They'll find us and they'll let us out. And they'll probably be nice enough not to tell anyone about it, if we ask them to keep it a secret.''

Felicia sighed. She was pouting as she said, ''I just hope you're right. In the meantime, I suppose all we can do is wait. Why don't we go sit in the Shoe Department? It's right over there. At least there are chairs over there. Besides,'' she added, sounding a little less grumpy, ''I might as well see if they have any shoes to go with the dress. I think black patent leather would be just the thing.''

Long after every single pair of shoes had been examined, however, no one showed up, no cleaning people, no security guards, not a single soul. Felicia was still concerned about word getting out about the girls' error, and so she insisted that they keep on waiting.

Susan, of course, was pleased. She didn't even mind following Felicia around the Shoe Department, listening to her comment on the pros and cons of every single pair of shoes on display.

Finally, Felicia announced, ''I'm getting bored.'' With a dramatic sigh, she dropped into one of the Shoe Department's chairs. ''I don't like any of these shoes, and I've already looked at sportswear, dresses, and jewelry. What's left? What can we possibly do now?''

"Well, we could go look around the Book Department,'' Susan suggested, trying to be helpful.

"It's too dark in here to read. Besides, I don't feel like it. In fact, all I feel like doing is getting out of this creepy place. Gosh, what are we going to *do* with ourselves all night?''

"We could just talk.''

Felicia looked at Susan as if she had just suggested they tap dance on the makeup counters.

"Talk?'' she repeated. "You and me *talk*? What could two people who are as different as we are *possibly* have to talk about?''

"I don't think we're so different, Felicia,'' said Susan. "I can see how you might think that. I mean, you're so outgoing and I am pretty quiet. You're always right in the middle of things, while I'm happiest when I'm off by myself, reading or painting. But despite all that, I really believe that, deep down, you and I really care about the same things.''

"Oh, really?'' Felicia sounded as if she were only half-listening. "Like what?''

"Like our friends. Our families. Doing the right thing.''

"I suppose.'' Felicia looked at her watch. "Gosh, it's barely seven o'clock. Are we going to be in here forever?''

"Just until the cleaning people show up,'' Susan reminded her, knowing full well that that wasn't about to happen for at least another twelve hours.

"Hmph." Felicia was silent for a long time. And then, much to Susan's surprise, she said, "Well, it's true that those things do mean a lot to me. My friends—my sorority sisters, especially—matter a lot. And my parents, especially my father, are extremely important to me.

"And then of course there's Clark." Her eyes were glowing as she said, "Wonderful, fabulous, stupendous Clark. Why, I'd do anything for him. Anything in the entire world."

"That's a real understatement," Susan replied without thinking.

Felicia bolted upright. "What did you mean by that, Susan Pratt?"

Susan was startled. "Why, I only meant that, uh, I know how much you, uh . . ."

All of a sudden, this whole pretense seemed absurd. Here she was, locked in a department store with a girl who could well hold the key to the very mystery that Susan and her twin were trying so hard to solve. Clark, Mr. Krigley, the mayor, and the threatening note he had received . . . and then there was Felicia, smack in the middle of it all. The temptation to find out exactly what the mayor's daughter knew was suddenly too great for Susan to resist.

"Felicia," she said hesitantly, "I have a small confession to make."

The other girl looked puzzled. "What are you talking about?"

"Earlier today, I overheard you and Clark talking. I don't want to go into the details of how, but I happen to know for a fact that he asked you to go on television and lie about Mr. Krigley being responsible for that threatening note that was sent to your father.''

"Why, it wasn't a lie! Clark is perfectly convinced that Mr. Krigley was responsible.''

"That's what Clark led you to believe, Felicia. You have no reason to believe him, though, not really. He wanted you to take what he was telling you on faith . . . plus he wanted you to say you had seen something that you hadn't really seen. Anyway,'' Susan couldn't resist adding, "I know Mr. Krigley. There's absolutely no way he could have sent that note. Aside from the fact that he's a harmless old man who just wants to be left alone, he's against the Old Woods Road development project, just like your father is. He *wanted* Mayor Harris to make that speech Friday night.

"Besides, I have some tangible proof.'' She went on to tell Felicia about the old man's misspelling of the word "business'' in the note she'd seen at his house— and the correct spelling of that same word in the threatening note that had been sent to the mayor.

"So what are you saying, that my boyfriend is a liar?'' Felicia demanded, her eyes flashing with anger.

"We both know that he asked you to lie,'' Susan replied gently. "That's not a very good sign, is it?''

"Well, I'm sure he had a good reason,'' Felicia insisted. "Just like when he asked me to make a copy of that key. . . .'' She stopped then, and her face turned as red as the display of red rubber boots on the shelf behind her.

"What key?'' Susan asked. The expression on her

face was one of dead seriousness. "What key are you talking about, Felicia?"

"It's none of your business." Felicia thrust her chin up into the air with her usual arrogance. But then, much to Susan's amazement, all of a sudden her face crumpled up and she began to cry.

"Oh, this whole thing is crazy," Felicia sobbed. "I never should have agreed to go along with it, but at the time it seemed perfectly innocent. It's just that I've been feeling so bad about it ever since."

Susan went over and sat down beside her. She got a tissue out of her skirt pocket and put a comforting arm around Felicia. "Here, blow your nose. And then tell me all about it. I guarantee it'll make you feel better."

"Well, I really don't see anything wrong with what I did—or at least I didn't at the time," Felicia said, blowing her nose and regaining some of her composure. "You see, my father has this secret filing cabinet that's always kept locked. He's the only one who has access to it. Even his assistants have never been allowed to go in there. He keeps all his notes inside, all his letters and memos, the speeches he's made or plans to make in the future. . . . Going into that filing cabinet is like going into his mind. At least, in terms of his role as mayor."

"Go on," Susan encouraged her in a soft voice.

"Anyway, this fall, a few weeks after Clark had started working for my father, he asked me for a date. I'd been crazy about him since the first time I laid eyes on him, so of course I said yes. He really seemed to like me, too. And then, on our third date, he asked me to prove that I really trusted him. He asked me to get him a copy of the key to that secret filing cabinet of my father's.''

She shrugged, then looked at Susan sheepishly. ''So I did.''

''I see.'' Susan tried not to sound critical. ''And how do you feel about it now?''

Felicia bit her lip, as if she were trying hard not to cry again. ''As much as I hate to admit it, I'm beginning to wonder if Clark has been using me to get to my father. First the key, and now wanting me to go on TV and lie about what I saw. . . .''

She turned to face Susan. ''What do *you* think?''

Susan thought for a long time, trying to come up with just the right thing to say.

''Felicia,'' she finally said, carefully measuring each of her words, ''I think this whole thing does sound suspicious. Of course you wanted to trust Clark. After all, he is your boyfriend. . . . But I can't help thinking that maybe your intuition is right. The first time could really have been an innocent request. But asking you to lie, on top of asking you for a way to get to the mayor's secret files . . . It does sound suspicious.''

Suddenly Felicia jumped up, out of her chair. ''That . . . that creep! Trying to hurt my father, and using me to do it. I'm going to get back at him for this.''

''Felicia, we're not completely certain about this.''

''*I* am. I couldn't possibly be more certain. All the pieces are starting to fit together now. All those 'late nights' when he was supposed to be working at City

Hall when everyone else had gone home, including my father; I bet that's when he did his spying. I wouldn't even be surprised if he had something to do with that threatening note. After all, lying about who was responsible was his idea. Why, I really believe that he's trying to make my father look bad.''

"But why on earth would he do that?"

"That, I'm afraid, I can't tell you. But I'm not going to let him get away with this any longer." She grabbed Susan's arm and started dragging her away. "Come on, Susan. Let's go."

"Where are we going?"

"We're getting out of here. I don't care who finds out about us getting locked in this store. This is too important to put off any longer. Now that I realize what kind of person Clark is, now that what has really been going on is clear to me, I'm going to find him and tell him exactly what I think of him. I'm going to tell my father, too. So there!"

Without giving Susan a chance to talk her out of her decision, Felicia raced toward the escalator, now unmoving, and dashed up to the telephones. Susan was right behind her, totally flabbergasted by this unexpected turn of events. She watched in silence as Felicia dialed the police.

"Hello, this is Felicia Harris, the mayor's daughter," Felicia said into the receiver. "I'm locked in Marbury's Department Store. No, I'm not alone. I'm with someone else . . . uh, a friend." She glanced over at Susan uncertainly before going on. "Can you send someone over to get us out of here right away?"

True to their promise, the police were there within

ten minutes. They led the two girls out of the store, explaining that they would have to notify the store manager and that he might want to talk to them at some later date. Otherwise, the two officers explained, they were free to go.

"By the way," one of them said as she walked the two girls to Susan's father's car, still parked in the mall parking lot, "it's a good thing you called when we did. Officer Murray and I were about to go out on another call. Felicia, you'll probably be interested in knowing that we caught the culprit who sent your father that threatening note last night. We were just going to get our paperwork together and then go out and arrest him."

"Really? That's good news!" Felicia looked at Susan with relief.

"It would have been a tough case if one of your father's assistants, Clark Rutherford, hadn't given us a tip. He said he was reluctant to come forward at first, but that in the end his conscience got the best of him, and he had to do what was right."

Felicia's expression darkened. "Oh, no. Who did he tell you was responsible?"

The police officer looked around. "Well, I probably shouldn't be telling you this, but you *are* the mayor's daughter. It was one of the residents of Old Woods Road. An old man by the name of Krigley."

"I see."

Felicia climbed into the car without saying another word. Once both girls were inside, however, alone and out of earshot, she turned to her and said, "Susan, what are we going to *do*? We know that the police are about to arrest an innocent man, but how can we stop them?''

''I know *exactly* how we can stop them.'' Susan turned the key in the ignition, put the car into gear, and headed out of the parking lot driving as fast as she dared. ''You and I are going to go right over to the WIT-TV station. Only this time, you're going on the air and tell the *truth*!''

Nine

Contrary to what Susan had told Felicia, the WIT-TV station was hopping. Not only were the producers, technicians, and newscasters all on hand for the on-going live coverage of Whittington High School's Homecoming Weekend, everyone there was excited about the tidbit of news that had just been leaked by the local police. They had just learned that the person responsible for the threatening note passed to the mayor the evening before had been identified and was about to be arrested.

"This is the biggest news we've had in weeks," Abby Preston was calling to one of the other WIT-TV employees as Felicia came rushing into the station. She was alone, having been dropped off at the front door by Susan. The parking lot was jammed with cars, and it was obvious that it was going to take a while to find a parking place. And by this point time was so precious that Susan hadn't wanted to waste another minute before setting Felicia loose inside the television station.

Felicia stood in the doorway, blinking in confusion as she tried to get herself oriented. All around her was a rush of activity. People were hurrying around the newsroom, talking on the telephone or typing hurriedly at word processors. Everyone there was obviously getting ready for an important event.

"We've got to be ready to put on a special report the instant that man is arrested." A newsperson that Felicia immediately recognized as Elaine Frank happened by, her cheeks flushed. She was talking to a small group of men and women who appeared to share her enthusiasm. "I want a film crew out at the house. I especially want shots of the old man being led out of his house in handcuffs.

"Then we'll cut to Mayor Harris and his reaction. We'll ask him the usual questions: how he feels about the police arresting the man who threatened him—"

"Excuse me," Felicia interrupted, a bit annoyed that her grand entrance had gone unnoticed. "I have something very important to—"

"Now let's get this whole thing organized," Elaine went on, ignoring her. "We haven't got much time."

"You don't seem to understand. I'm—"

"I'm sorry, Miss, but you'll have to wait." Abby cast her a sharp look. "Can't you see that we're very busy?"

"But you're wrong! Old Mr. Krigley is *not* responsible for sending the mayor that threatening note."

Abby just looked at her. "Are you saying that the police are wrong?"

Felicia stuck her chin up in the air. "I, for one, happen to have firsthand knowledge that the person who claims to have seen Mr. Krigley pass that note to the mayor is lying. And I'm willing to go on TV and announce it publicly."

"Hah! Who do you think you are, anyway, the Queen of Sheba?"

"As a matter of fact," Felicia said with an arrogant toss of her head, "I'm Felicia Harris. Mayor Harris's daughter."

Abby and Elaine looked at each other and burst out laughing.

"Right," said Abbey. "You're Felicia Harris, and I'm Cleopatra."

"And I'm Marie Antoinette." Elaine chuckled. "Now look, whoever you are. We get cranks like you coming in here all the time, pretending they have something to say just so they can be on television. Everybody wants to be on TV, and people will make up any story in order to get their faces plastered across the screen."

"But I *am* Felicia Harris!" Felicia was confused. This was like a bad dream. "The story I have to tell is one hundred percent true! I *know* Clark Rutherford, the person who told the police that Mr. Krigley is responsible for that note. I know he's a liar. Why, he even asked me to lie for him, to tell everyone that I saw Mr. Krigley pass that note to my father when in reality I never saw anything at all."

"If that's the case, Miss Whoever-you-are, why don't you just go down to the police station and tell them what you know?"

"Because they'd never believe me. Look, even *you* don't believe me. At this point, the only way to stop the police from going ahead and arresting Mr. Krigley is to get public sympathy on the old man's side. The police couldn't possibly go ahead and arrest him if the mayor's daughter had just gone on TV and told all of Whittington that she knows for a fact that the supposed 'witness' is a liar!"

"Look," said Abby. She was obvious growing tired of this whole conversation. "You're right; the police couldn't very well arrest an innocent man if a credible witness had appeared on TV minutes before, saying he was innocent. It would make a great story, and I'd put it on in a minute. But only if we could get the *real* mayor's daughter to go on TV and tell it—"

"But I *am* the real mayor's daughter!" Felicia cried. "You've got to believe me."

"Wait a minute. *There's* the mayor's daughter!" Elaine was pointing toward the doorway, right behind Felicia. The entire room grew silent, and all eyes turned in the same direction.

"Sorry I took so long," Susan said as she came rushing in. "It took me forever to find a parking space. I ended up way over—"

She stopped in mid sentence, having just realized that the whole room full of people was staring at her.

"Hello, Felicia," said Elaine. "It's nice to see you again. By the way, is this girl a friend of yours?"

"Well, uh, yes, she is." Susan was still struggling

to make some sense out of all the apparent confusion.

"Then I suggest that you have a nice long chat with her and straighten her out," Elaine went on with a smile. "She seems to be going through some sort of identity crisis."

"Susan," said Felicia, "I don't know what's going on here, but these people refuse to believe that I'm Felicia Harris."

"That's right," Abby said matter-of-factly. "Maybe that's because we can see for ourselves that the *real* Felicia Harris is standing two feet away from you."

"Now, what brings you here, Felicia?" she asked, turning to face Susan. "Have you come to make a statement about the impending arrest of the man who threatened your father?"

"Wait a minute. I'm not . . . you see, this really is . . . I mean, I don't . . ."

And then she stopped talking. Suddenly what was happening became clear to her. And it all made perfect sense. Just a few hours earlier, Chris had shown up at the TV station, claiming to be Felicia Harris. There had been no reason for the people here not to believe her, and she had gone on the air, playing the role of the mayor's daughter.

And now, a girl with the exact same face as Chris's showed up at the television station once again.

Now that she had figured it all out, Susan wasn't about to let a golden opportunity pass.

"Yes, I'm Felicia Harris. And I want to go on TV right now and announce publicly that I know for a fact that the police are about to arrest the wrong person.

There's a big scandal behind this, a story about a man named Clark Rutherford who took a job as the mayor's assistant, then proceeded to spy on him, to work toward making him look bad, and—as if all that weren't already enough—to get the mayor's daughter involved in trying to discredit him. All the while he was plotting to bring down another man as well: poor, innocent Mr. Krigley. And I intend to go on television and expose this whole terrible conspiracy.''

"Are you ready to go on right now?'' asked Abby excitedly.

"The sooner the better. Every second counts. We have to get on the air before the police get over to Mr. Krigley's house. I'm more than ready. Just show me where to go.''

As Abby and Elaine led Susan away, toward the studio, Felicia called out, ''But *I'm* the mayor's daughter!''

But no one paid her the slightest bit of attention.

"I wanted to go public with this story before an innocent person had to go through the trauma of being arrested,'' Susan said, turning to face the television camera with the glowing red light.

"I want to thank you, Ms. Frank, for giving me the chance to go on the air and stop this before it goes any further. I know the poor old man who was almost a victim in this whole affair would have been very upset if he had been unjustly arrested. And he never would have recovered from all the bad publicity that would have surrounded him, even after his name had been cleared.''

"It's very brave of you to come forth with this story," said Elaine Frank, "but there are still so many unanswered questions. Why was Clark Rutherford asking you to lie for him, Felicia? What exactly was he hoping to accomplish by trying to discredit your father? Was he working for someone—and if so, who? In other words, what's the *real* story behind all this?"

"Uh, I, uh . . ."

For once, Susan was totally tongue-tied. The more she spoke, exposing the story behind Clark and the threatening note, the more questions there appeared to be. And the truth of the matter was that she just didn't have the answers.

She was trying to decide what to say next, knowing that hundreds, maybe thousands, of viewers were in their living rooms, waiting to hear her answer. But her mind was a complete blank.

And then, all of a sudden, she noticed someone sneaking into the studio. She could make out the silhouette of a young woman who was carrying a white piece of paper, heading toward the platform on which Susan and Elaine were sitting.

It was Chris!

"Ms. Frank, I'm afraid I don't have the answers to those questions. But I know someone who just may. Here she comes now."

The interviewer looked over and saw Chris coming toward them. And then her face registered shock.

"Wait a minute!" she cried. "It's . . . you're . . . how. . . ?" She blinked in confusion, then said, "I never knew the mayor had *twin daughters*!"

Chris and Susan looked at each other, and then they both burst out laughing.

"Ms. Frank," said Chris, "I'd say we have a lot of explaining to do. Not only about the scandal over at City Hall, but also about some of the little tricks my twin sister and I used to uncover it.

"But first, let's get Felicia Harris—that is, the *real* Felicia Harris— in here. We have a long story to tell, one that I'm certain your viewers are going to find very interesting. But I think what we need to do is go back and start at the beginning."

Ten

The final event of the weekend, Sunday evening's Homecoming dance, was already in full swing by the time Susan and Chris arrived. The Whittington High School gym looked more like something out of a dream than a place for playing basketball and volleyball. Katy's sister Kelly and a crackerjack team of seniors had put their heads together, rolled up their sleeves, and worked long hours—and the results were striking.

Crêpe paper streamers in vibrant shades of orange, yellow, and brown were hung everywhere, punctuated by huge clusters of balloons in the same colors. The lighting had been softened to make the room much more romantic. Centerpieces of yellow and white chrysanthemums sat on the round tables that had been set up near the refreshments: hot, spicy apple cider and fresh cinnamon doughnuts. Just about everybody in town had shown up; at least that was the conclusion Chris drew as she and her sister maneuvered their way through the crowd.

"Goodness, Sooz, didn't anybody stay at home tonight?" she joked, yelling in order to be heard over the loud rock band that was playing.

"It's a good thing for all of us that the people in this town like to go out and have fun," Susan countered. "There wouldn't have been such a happy ending to the Lollipop Plot if they were the type who liked to stay home and watch TV all day—like on Saturday afternoon, when you were on television, passing yourself off as the mayor's daughter! But then again, it's fortunate for us that a lot of them *do* like to watch TV on a Saturday *night*."

Chris laughed. She had to admit that her sister had a good point—and that she was perfectly correct when she referred to the Lollipop Plot as having had a "happy ending."

As far as the twins were concerned, it had been a complete success. The timely appearance of their television report had indeed kept the police from arresting Mr. Krigley. In fact, the entire town was up in arms the instant the special report was aired on WIT-TV, with Susan, Chris, and Felicia exposing the true story behind the mysterious threatening note that had been sent to the mayor. The telephones at both the television station and the police station began ringing nonstop. And in the end it was not old Mr. Krigley who received a visit from two police officers with arrest warrants in their hands; it was both Alfred J. Pierce and his sidekick, Clarkson P. Rutherford III.

As the twins neared the stage on which the band was playing, the music suddenly stopped. A hush fell over the crowd. And then, all at once, everyone in the room broke into loud cheering and enthusiastic applause.

"Three cheers for Chris and Susan!" someone called out.

And then there was the unanimous cry, "Hip-hip-hooray! Hip-hip-hooray! Hip-hip-hooray!"

At that point Mayor Harris emerged from the crowd. He came over to the girls and put one arm around each of them.

"Speech! Speech!" someone else demanded.

The mayor motioned for the girls to join him up on the stage. When the crowd had settled down, he began to speak.

"Christine, Susan, I want to congratulate you both for getting to the bottom of that threatening note that was passed to me on Friday night—and uncovering the plot behind it. You helped the police identify the people who were trying to discredit me, mainly in order to push through a land development project that would have hurt the entire town of Whittington, especially some of its more elderly residents.

"And, on a more personal level," he added, his eyes twinkling merrily, "I owe you both my heartfelt gratitude for putting an end to this terrible mystery. I can assure you that I didn't enjoy the feeling that someone out there was sending me anonymous threats."

The crowd began to cheer once again, not stopping until the mayor held up his hands for silence.

"There's someone else who owes you a thank-you, too," he went on. "Felicia, where are you?"

A low murmur filled the room as the people of Whittington waited for the mayor's daughter to emerge from the crowd. When she did, she strode up to the stage, her chin held high in the air. And then, just for effect, she tossed her head, a motion which sent ripples of light through her thick mane of blond hair.

"I suppose you did a fine job and all that," she said loftily. "Helping my father was a very good deed. But one thing's for sure," she said, her eyes flashing as she turned to face Susan. "It's going to be a long, long time before I set foot in Marbury's Department Store again!"

There was laughter and more applause. The group on the stage was about to climb down once again. But they suddenly stopped when someone else began to speak.

"Wait a minute! Hold on, there! There's somebody else who wants to thank the Pratt twins!" came one more voice from deep in the crowd, a voice that wasn't readily recognizable by anyone. "Let me through, let me through. I have something I want to say."

An old man made his way forward, with people politely moving aside to let him pass. He was dressed in a suit and tie, his clothing threadbare but neat and well cared for. Most noticeable, however, were his bright, lively blue eyes. Many people gasped as they realized that the man they were seeing was somebody who hadn't ventured into their midst for over a decade.

"I want to thank these girls for taking the time to help out an old man," Mr. Krigley said once he had reached the bandstand. "Chris, Susan, not only did you keep me from being unjustly accused of doing something as low as sending a threatening note to our fine mayor here." He patted Mayor Harris on the back. "You also helped us residents of Old Woods Road fight that preposterous plan to knock down our precious homes to make room for still one more shopping center, surely the very last thing this town needs."

"Yes, Susan and Chris did a commendable job," the mayor agreed heartily. "Now, what do you say we get on with this Homecoming dance of ours and all go back to having a good time?"

The music resumed as the foursome climbed off the stage. The band sounded wonderful, even though one of its members had chosen to sit this one out, as Chris quickly discovered.

"Why, Todd," she said after she had reached the dance floor and felt someone tap her on the shoulder.

"Care to dance?" he asked with a grin. "I happen to know that this band is first-rate, so we might as well enjoy their music."

"It sounds like a great idea to me."

Susan, meanwhile, was standing alone, watching the dancers and listening to the music, when her friend Katy happened by.

"My, my, I haven't seen you for a long time," Katy teased. "So tell me, Susan, have you gotten yourself locked into any interesting department stores lately?"

"Why, yes, I have, as a matter of fact, thanks to you," Susan returned, laughing. "By the way, Katy, I want to thank you for helping me out last night. If it hadn't been for the information you gave me about the store's routine for closing up, I never would have been able to keep Felicia out of the way long enough for Chris to get to the bottom of all this."

"Well, I want to thank you, too—on my sister Kelly's behalf."

"Kelly?" Susan was puzzled. "Why would she want to thank me?"

"For giving her the idea for the perfect Senior Class project. Starting next week, the seniors of Whittington High are going to take turns volunteering to help the older residents in town, like the people out on Old Woods Road, take care of their homes. Mowing lawns, shoveling snow, raking leaves, even painting . . . all the tasks that are simply too much for our senior citizens to handle by themselves.

"The seniors are also going to be raising money to buy the supplies they'll need. As a matter of fact, they're starting tonight."

"Really? What's their plan?"

Katy turned around and scanned the crowd. And then she pointed to someone making her way across the room, carrying a huge cardboard box.

"Here comes Kelly now," she said with a grin. "I'll let her show you what the senior class is going to be selling tonight as part of their new fund-raising campaign."

By that point, Kelly had reached Susan and Katy.

She immediately flipped open the box, revealing a burst of bright color—red and yellow and orange and green.

"Look what I've got," she said triumphantly. "Hundreds and hundreds of lollipops, donated by Marbury's Department Store."

"Selling lollipops," Susan said with a smile. "What a wonderful idea. And I'll bet my sister with the sweet tooth will be your very first customer. It's a wonderful idea, and I'm really glad that Chris and I helped your sister think of it."

"Excuse me," somebody interrupted, "but are you too busy talking to take some time out to dance?"

Susan turned and found Adam Leeds standing beside her.

"After all," he went on, "this *is* a dance. And what else are you supposed to do at a dance . . . but dance?"

"You're pretty persuasive," Susan said with a chuckle. "I can see that you're a real asset to your college's debating team. How could I possibly reject logic like that?"

She turned to her friend. "Katy, do you mind?"

"Not at all," Katy replied with an impish grin. "Especially since I'm eager to watch *this*."

Susan and Adam turned to see what Katy was talking about. There was Felicia, just a few feet away. At the moment, she was trying to discourage old Mr. Krigley, who kept insisting that she dance with him.

"Really," she was protesting, "I don't think I—"

"Don't be shy," Mr. Krigley said. "I know we

only just met, you and me, but what better way is there to become friends?''

Felicia glanced around, looking for someone to rescue her. But there was no one to help. "I'd like to, Mr. Krigley, really I would, but, uh—"

"Oh, I get it. Not much of a dancer, huh? Well, then, maybe I can teach you a thing or two. You know, back in my day, I cut quite a figure out on the dance floor. It's easy once you get the hang of it. Come on, I'll show you.''

With that, Mr. Krigley whirled the astonished Felicia across the room, her long hair swinging behind her as she struggled to keep up with him.

Susan caught her twin sister's eye. The two girls immediately burst out laughing at the sight of poor Felicia doing an energetic two-step with old Mr. Krigley. He, meanwhile, looked as if he couldn't be happier. In fact, he was quite a different person from the one the Pratts had visited just the day before.

Susan sighed. She wondered if it would turn out that she and Chris had accomplished even more over this Homecoming Weekend than they thought.

And then she turned back to the young man at her side.

"Now, Adam," Susan said with a flirtatious grin. "How about that dance?''

About the Author

Cynthia Blair grew up on Long Island, earned her B.A. from Bryn Mawr College in Pennsylvania, and went on to get an M.S. in marketing from M.I.T. She worked as a marketing manager for food companies but now has abandoned the corporate life in order to write. She lives on Long Island with her husband and her son.